INTO THE CHILLING WATER

December 2007

To Marti
with love,

Joe Dickey

Also by Joe Richard Morgan

Potato Branch: Sketches of Mountain Memories

INTO THE
CHILLING
WATER

JOE RICHARD MORGAN

Ridgetop Books
Fairview, North Carolina

Printed in the United States of America

Cover photograph by Michael Bruckner

Ridgetop Books is an imprint of Bright Mountain Books, Inc.

Printed in the United States of America

ISBN-10: 0-914875-51-5
ISBN-13: 978-0-914875-51-2

Library of Congress Cataloging-in-Publication Data

Morgan, Joe Richard, 1934–
  Into the chilling water / Joe Richard Morgan.
    p. cm.
  Summary: "Short stories based on the author's youth in the rural Appalachian mountains during the 1930s, 1940s, and 1950s. Set on Potato Branch, now called Morgan Branch, in Buncombe County, North Carolina, these stories describe crops and livestock, logging, moonshine, racial tensions, and general family life."—Provided by publisher.
    ISBN-13: 978-0-914875-51-2 (pbk. : alk. paper)
    ISBN-10: 0-914875-51-5 (pbk. : alk. paper)
    1. Country life—Appalachian Region—Fiction. 2. Appalachian Region—Rural conditions—Fiction. 3. Buncombe County (N.C.)—Fiction. I. Title.
  PS3613.O7445I67 2007
  813'.6—dc22

                                              2007038766

In memory of Ellie
(Cora Estelle Daves)
1880–1963

and for
Milli, Andrea, Sarah, and Jonathan

Contents

Part One

Grandfather and the Sheriff 3

Part Two

Into the Chilling Water 13
Senseless Things 18
In the Shade 21
Sleep Tight 25
A Miracle 29
The Bucket of Cold Water 35
Under the Blazing Sun 38

Part Three

The Whip Spoke 45
The Witch and the Well 54
The Real Thing 60
Stopped in His Tracks 71
The Whole Earth 75

Part Four

The Gun in Dad's Hands 79
Slaughter Time 84
Alone in the Woods with Kate 90
During Snowflakes 95
His Last Letter 105
Welcome to the South 111
The Shadow of Death 115
Burn-scarred Hands 119

About the Author 123

Preface

Set in the North Carolina mountains, these stories from the 1930s, 1940s, and 1950s form a final farewell to those "giants" of my earth who are now "sleeping on the hill."

—JRM

Acknowledgments

My gratitude to Lyn and Harry Fozzard for their on-going interest in the art of Carolina writers; to Liz Guy, professional storyteller, for her keen sense of structure and historical accuracy; to Ann Dobbins, poet and teacher, for her friendship and companionship in writing; to Doris Wenzel, publisher, for her sound editorial advice and friendship; to Cynthia Bright, editor, friend, and publisher, who took a chance with my first book; and to Milli, my wife and best friend.

Also I acknowledge the thousands of readers of my first collection, *Potato Branch: Sketches of Mountain Memories,* who have insisted on a few more sketches from my pen.

Now, Muses, now, high Genius, do your part!
And Memory, faithful scrivener to the eyes,
Here show thy virtue, noble as thou art!

Dante Alighieri
Inferno. II.7–9
Commedia

PART ONE

GRANDFATHER AND THE SHERIFF

The day Aunt Lura celebrated her ninety-second birthday, she told me, "Lawrence Brown, the sheriff, and his revenuers came many times and searched for your grandfather's still, but they never, ever found it." She laughed and added, "The sheriff was always reminding people that *the law* was in LAWrence."

Grandfather Joe Anders was a man of many talents. He owned the forty-eight acres of mountains he farmed, but he was primarily an ironmonger, blacksmith, and farrier. His main forge was built on his mountain estate. He broke and trained draft animals (oxen and mules), grew sugar cane and made molasses (sorghum) for sale. A skilled craftsman, he made the furniture and caned the chairs that filled my grandparents' home. As architect-carpenter, he designed and built the large, log home into which he moved his family one year before his untimely death.

Grandfather also distilled the whiskey he needed. The late 1800s and early 1900s was an age before aspirin, penicillin, and modern medicine. Pure corn whiskey was an essential ingredient in demand for many home remedies. Alcohol was, and still is, an effective disinfectant for a wound as well as a good anesthetic for pain, and a large dose of whiskey can render one unconscious as well as insensitive. For the mountain farmer, home-manufactured whiskey was also a source of cash income for buying sugar, calico, gunpowder, and for paying his taxes.

Grandfather doctored his children at home, using only home remedies. When one of my cousins badly burned her hand in a open fire, Grandfather wrapped each finger separately in a bandage, then saturated the bandages with linseed oil. When her hand healed she had no scars.

"When your Uncle Homer contracted pneumonia as a teenager," Aunt Lura told me, "Daddy sat beside Homer's bed with a jar of his whiskey, caring for Homer and waiting for the crisis." It was a time when pneumonia usually took its victim to the grave. When the crisis came, Grandfather raised Homer up in his arms to a sitting position in the bed and forced several spoonfuls of his whiskey down him. The fever broke and my Uncle regained his health.

"It was in 1917," Aunt Lura remembered, "when we lived in Canton, that typhoid fever broke out in the city. Cattle grazing on the Canton watershed died with blackleg. Those animals contaminated the city water." Grandfather moved his family out of Haywood County across the mountain into the great Newfound Valley of Buncombe County where he later met and outwitted Sheriff Lawrence Brown.

In Grandfather's day, a home whiskey distillery

included a small furnace with a firebox and a good drawing flu; a copper cooker, which is the still itself; a worm, which is a ¾-inch copper pipe coiled tightly and placed in a fifty-gallon barrel through which cold water was constantly circulated; a good supply of cold, fresh water; and, of course, a foolproof hiding place.

The corn mash was first made into a beer from which the alcohol was distilled. When the alcohol first flowed out of the end of the worm, it was then strained through hickory coals to remove the fusel oils or "barda grease." The spent beer was drained from the copper cooker and fed to the hogs, as they particularly love corn mash. To refine the whiskey to the ultimate, the alcohol was run through the still a second time, condensing the steam again into alcohol before it flowed through a strainer and funneled into the container or whiskey jar. This process took a long day of constant attention by the distiller.

How did Grandfather run and conceal his still from the man who thought the law resided in his name?

ๆ๛◆๛

For the first years on the mountain farm, my grandparents' home was essentially one long, large room with a fireplace at one end. The kitchen was attached at the side of the house. The family grew to twelve members that included Grandfather's half-sister, my great-aunt Sarah, who was handicapped by a stroke. They all lived in the one-room house and slept in the back part away from the fireplace.

"We ate in the kitchen on the long table Daddy made," Aunt Lura explained. "Mama always had a stove, but she cooked many things in the fireplace: potatoes banked in the ashes, cornbread in the Dutch oven, water or vegetables boiled in an iron pot that hung above the fire on an arm that swung out from the firewall."

About seventy feet from the kitchen door there was a spring of pure, clear, cold water, the essential in distilling whiskey. The water sprung from the foot of the mountain and flowed through its grass-covered stream to pour over a low waterfall just outside the kitchen door. From there it flowed over the great rock of the kitchen yard and cascaded down into the branch. The branch rushed down from the high mountain pasture of Grandfather's land and flowed into Newfound Creek far down the valley.

Over thousands of years that spring water had worn its bed across the huge granite rock that became my grandparents' kitchen yard. Long before Europeans knew of the American continent, generations and tribes of Cherokees had camped and hunted there and drank of the pure, cold waters. Wolves whelped in the laurels and rhododendron that shelter the spring. Cougars or mountain lions, which the early settlers called painters, prowled those hills and often took a newborn calf from bison or elk that once frequented the spring. Bears fed on the chestnuts, acorns, blackberries and huckleberries, chinquapins, and the honey they found in gum trees during their summers of feasting.

In the Anders Cove, as it came to be called, game was plentiful. Wild turkeys, woodchucks, rabbits, deer, elk, racoons, possum, and polecats abounded. There was an orchard of ancient, dead, chestnut trees standing on the land when Grandfather bought it. He felled the trees and, with his own saws, milled the logs into lumber. He hauled it by wagon over Newfound Mountain to Canton where he sold it.

When Grandfather went for the cows before milking time or into the fields, he often carried his rifle. Once he shot a fox traveling across his path, unknown to him, being pursued by hounds. When the hunters with their dogs arrived, they took Grandfather to court for killing the fox before their hounds. There was some holdover of an English law that forbade killing a fox, even on one's own land, before fox hunters' hounds.

Grandmother raised guinea fowl, pheasantlike birds with blackish plumage marked with many small white spots; bantam chickens, and hogs. I remember her large vegetable garden with its section for rhubarb and herbs. Grandfather built a picket fence around the garden to keep the rabbits and chickens out. He built a large, log smokehouse between the spring stream and the vegetable garden. His smokehouse bordered the kitchen yard and stood above the high bank of the mountain branch. He built a two-seater outhouse over the branch just below the smokehouse.

Grandmother's wash pot was located on the kitchen side of the yard beside the spring and the woodshed.

The clotheslines stretched along the path toward the spring. I remember the row of beehives Grandfather set up in the tall grass on the house side of the path leading to the spring.

Aunt Lura told me, "When your mother was a small child, she wandered up to the front of one of the hives and stood in the tall grass. Daddy saw his small daughter standing there in the wet grass and saw her being covered with bees. He picked her up at the waist with both hands and swung her face down back and forth in the tall grass to brush the honey bees off her face and arms. She didn't suffer a single sting."

Grandfather built the milk race over the spring stream in the shade of surrounding gum trees, laurel, and rhododendron at the spring. It was a wonderful natural refrigeration for milk, cheese, and butter. The cold, spring water ran under and around the bottom of the food containers twenty-four hours every day of the year. I could appreciate it as a boy that no one had to pump well-water to fill the milk race twice a day as I had to do at home.

ᴄᴏ◆ᴄᴏ

"My younger siblings did not know that Daddy made whiskey," Aunt Lura told me.

How did he keep it secret from the younger children and secure from the lawmen?

"He didn't talk about it." Aunt Lura paused and remembered. "Mama told me about a time Daddy hid his jars of whiskey between some rows in the cornfield.

We grew corn all the way up that mountain on the other side of the branch. You'd never believe it today the way that place is grown up in trees. We had a tomato patch right on top of that mountain once, the best tomatoes we ever had."

She looked away seeing in her memory a mountain cornfield over seventy-five years past. "He forgot where he had placed his jars in the field, and when he came into the house he was very upset. Mama took him back up the hill, climbing straight to the spot, and showed him where he had hid his whiskey. Your grandmother always watched out for your grandfather.

"Whenever Lawrence Brown and the Federal men came, they hunted everywhere, even in the kitchen," Aunt Lura related. "One time Mama and I were canning blackberries in glass, gallon jars, and Mama had about twelve jars sealed and standing in the corner. The sheriff kept looking at the jars of blackberries. He'd pick each one up and examine it carefully and then put it down. He seemed to think that they could somehow be whiskey. I don't know why he spent so much time with those jars.

"Sheriff Lawrence Brown was a rude and arrogant man," Aunt Lura suddenly digressed. "He wandered through the house opening closets and looking into cabinets, never respecting anyone's privacy. It was known that he would confiscate a man's whiskey and then bootleg it himself. He was re-elected over and over. I don't know why people thought him a good sheriff."

Aunt Lura rested a moment and then added, "Mama and I continued canning berries and he quit the kitchen."

ço ♦ ९

As a smith, Grandfather, of course, made copper cookers and worms for those who needed a still. As a farmer, Grandfather had the corn, and Grandmother had the corn mash for her hungry hogs.

But where did he find the foolproof hiding place for his distillery?

"Remember that old, log, smokehouse?" Aunt Lura smiled at me. "Remember those thick, floor planks? They were not nailed down."

Underneath the smokehouse, entered only by removing some of the floor boards, Grandfather had a basement in which he placed his distillery. The endless supply of fresh, cold, pure, spring water he piped into the basement. Via the drain pipe, gravity carried the water out of the basement and into the branch running under the two-seater outhouse. Grandfather could smoke hams and distill whiskey at the same time.

Sheriff Brown spent his time searching the log cabin, the milk race, and the forge where there was a furnace. Grandfather understood the Lawrence Browns of the world. Grandfather was no fool.

PART TWO

Into the Chilling Water

At the water's edge, the choir sang *a cappella*:

> *Shall we gather at the river,*
> *where bright angel feet have trod;*
> *with its crystal tide forever*
> *flowing by the throne of God?*

We were not standing by a river. In the tall grass, I didn't see any tracks of bright angel feet. The tide, however, was crystal clear. I looked at the smooth stones and pebbles deep in the bottom of Newfound Creek. The "tide" was flowing pretty steadily and I knew it to be cold. It flowed, not by the throne of God, but under several weeping willows that leaned out over the stream, shading part of that icy water from the warm sunshine.

From distant mountains surrounding the valley, tributaries bubbling from numberless natural springs splashed their waters over rocks and rapids to swell the great creek. From the Bear Wallow Gap the creek had added waters from the Anders Cove, Morgan Branch, Hayes Cove, Brooks Branch, and many other mountain streams.

In the Newfound Valley far beyond where we stood, more tributaries would add many waters to the creek, which itself would become a tributary to the French Broad River. The Cherokee peoples named the river Long Man. The Cherokee saw it fed by the Long Man's Chattering Children, all the brooks and rivulets winding through the mountains. For a section of rapids below Asheville, the Cherokee called the river Tahkeeosteh, meaning *where they race*. I thought of the Cherokee who, for centuries before we stood by the Creek, had also used these waters in cleansing ceremonies.

The French Broad River, called so because it is a broad river and because the French were the first Europeans to have settled it, would gather the waters of a hundred creeks, the Big Pigeon River, the Nolichucky River, and the Holston River. At Knoxville, the French Broad River would become the Tennessee River. On it would flow, through north Alabama and west Tennessee and west Kentucky and into the great Ohio River. By that route the water of Newfound Creek would flow on into the great Mississippi River and into the Gulf of Mexico and finally into the Atlantic Ocean.

> *On the bosom of the river*
> *where the Savior-King we own,*
> *we shall meet, and sorrow never,*
> *'neath the glory of the throne.*

Pastor of Zion Hill Baptist Church, my Uncle Bud Mehaffey, fully dressed in his Sunday suit, waded to the center of the creek. He stood deep in the stream, trembling a bit from the cold mountain water. Holding his well-worn Bible in his hands, Uncle Bud read loudly selections from the Gospel of Matthew:

> In those days came John the Baptist, preaching in the wilderness of Judea, and saying, Repent ye: for the kingdom of heaven is at hand. . . Then went out to him Jerusalem, and all Judea, and all the region round about Jordan, and were baptized of him in Jordan, confessing their sins. . . Then cometh Jesus from Galilee to Jordan unto John, to be baptized of him. . . And Jesus, when he was baptized, went up straightway out of the waters: and, lo, the heavens were opened unto him, and he saw the Spirit of God descending in the body of a dove, and lighting upon him: And lo, a voice from heaven, saying, This is my beloved Son, in whom I am well pleased.

> *Ere we reach the shining river,*
> *lay we every burden down;*
> *grace our spirits will deliver,*
> *and provide a robe and crown.*

After taking a few slow and careful steps against the current, Uncle Bud handed his Bible to Aunt Estelle who stood at the water's edge. He held out his hand to my best friend, Don Rogers, the first person ahead of me in the line of new converts who were joining Zion Hill Baptist Church.

Don and Uncle Bud waded down into the center of the creek, Don trying not to show how the icy water climbing up his legs and around his crotch chilled him.

Watching Don, I recalled one Sunday afternoon one year before when Don took me up the branch above my Grandmother Anders' home to show me the swimming hole he had helped make by damming up the mountain stream in the pasture. Not having any bathing suits, and being alone, we took off all our clothes and jumped into the chilling water. After only a few splashes, we heard the voices of our sisters, female cousins, and mothers coming up the trail. Before they approached within sight, Don and I climbed out of the frigid water and pulled our clothes back on over our wet bodies.

Uncle Bud crossed Don's hands against Don's chest, placed his left hand at the nape of Don's neck, raised his right hand high in the air toward heaven, and said, "I baptize you, Don, in the name of the Father, the Son, and the Holy Ghost. Amen."

Immediately, Uncle Bud placed his right hand on Don's hands and lowered Don backwards and under the water. When Uncle Bud lifted him back up, Don fought for his balance and wiped the water from his face with both hands, gasped for breath, and shook himself against the cold. As Uncle Bud held Don's arm and led him to the shore, Don's light, blue, cotton trousers clung skin-tight to his legs and crotch. I thought of when we were naked climbing out of the swimming hole.

Into the Chilling Water

Don's father took Don's hand as he stepped quivering onto the bank. His mother wrapped him in a robe.

Yes, we'll gather at the river,
the beautiful, the beautiful river;
gather with the saints at the river,
that flows by the throne of God.

Uncle Bud reached for my hand.

Senseless Things

The four o'clock city bus from downtown Asheville eased to a stop in West Asheville. It was heavily loaded, passengers standing from front to back. Several people worked their way off the bus before it pulled back into traffic, but Mother was not among them.

"Your mother must have missed the bus," Dad said. He and I had been waiting for her at the Winn-Dixie. "She wants to get some groceries before we head home," he explained.

In a short while we saw another city bus, headed back toward Asheville, come to its stop across the road from the market. When it pulled away into traffic, there stood Mother watching for her chance to cross the street.

"I'm a little late," she said as she came closer to us, "because of an incident on the bus."

"What happened?" I asked. Mother looked at Dad.

"At the stop down by the river a little colored lad got on, about eight or ten years old. The bus was very crowded, people standing thick in the aisle. I was standing near the front pressed close to people with all our shopping bags."

"What about the boy?" Dad wanted to know.

"He was alone and after he put his nickel in the glass, he got around the first two men but had to stop by me where there was no room to pass.

"The driver was watching him in his rear-view, and when the child stopped by me, the driver said loudly, 'Boy, you know you belong in the back. Get movin'.'

"I couldn't just stand there, so I put an arm around the child who was shaking with fear, and I said to the driver, 'Can't you see this child can't get through this crowd? Your job is to drive the bus. I will care for this boy.'"

Dad smiled at Mother and asked, "Then what?"

"Well, he drove on, and I told the child, 'You're just fine here with me,' and I kept my arm around him and held to a seat corner with one hand. I could feel the hostility around me in the way some people looked at me with hard stares, so I knew that I should not abandon that child by getting off the bus before he did."

Mother took a deep breath looking at Dad and continued, "I decided to stay on the bus and get off at his stop with him, which I did. I got a transfer when we got off and I crossed the street and caught the next bus back to you."

Dad grinned and said, "We better get our groceries and get home before milking time."

In the market, while Mother was grinding the JFG coffee beans for our percolator, I recalled a time when I was younger with Dad at the Sears store then on Cox Avenue in Asheville.

We had gone to the water fountain on the ground floor and I had asked Dad, "Is one fountain for women and the other for men? Why are there two fountains?" He had explained that the signs over the fountains read "Colored" on the left one and "White" on the right one. Of course, he also explained that the "Colored" one was for blacks and the "White" fountain was for us.

Not letting it go, I had asked Dad if the water was different in the fountains and could I taste the "Colored" water. He had said, "Go ahead." It never occurred to me then that a black person caught drinking from the "White" fountain would probably be arrested and punished.

When I announced that the water tasted the same from both fountains, Dad laughed and pointed out the water pipe below the fountains. It ran straight from one fountain to the other. Dad had said, "Son, you will learn that this is just one of the senseless things of our time."

In the Winn-Dixie, mother poured the coffee beans into the grinder. I smelled the freshly ground coffee.

IN THE SHADE

"The chain gang's coming," my father announced as the screen door shut behind him. He had just arrived home from the gristmill in Leicester. He was carrying a sack of flour that he took upstairs to the large wooden barrel where my parents stored flour and corn meal to keep it dry and safe from mice, ants, and weevils.

As Dad came back downstairs and through the kitchen Mother asked, "Where is the chain gang?"

"They're trimming the bank just this side of Harry's," Dad answered. "The guard asked me if it is still all right for the trustee to get water here, and I told him 'sure.'" It was common for groups of prisoners under guard to appear in late August trimming the hedges of our rural road.

It wasn't long after Dad drove his Roadster back to Grandfather Morgan's garage where he kept it, that the trustee appeared in our yard and asked Mother if he could fill his water bucket at our pump. It was a bright sky-blue August morning that promised a hot day and constant trips of the trustee to our well for water.

The second time he arrived in our yard, Mother asked him his name and how many men there were in his group, and she told the trustee to tell the guard

21

that the men could eat their lunch on our lawn under the shade trees. Then she added, "Ask your guard if it would be all right if I bake a pie and a cake for the men to add to their dinner."

The trustee's face brightened and he said, "That'd be mighty kind of you, Mrs. Morgan. I'll tell the guard."

That was enough for Mother to send me to the woodyard for dry wood to add to the hot coals in the kitchen stove. My sisters, the twins, who were two years younger than I, got to lick the cake bowls. I fetched the apples for the pie. Mother kept us busy at some chore while she cooked and baked.

I asked, "Are you going to bake enough for all the convicts?"

"They're just boys," she quipped. "And I'm sure they all miss their home and good cooking."

Mother gave us strict orders: "Don't run in telling me about prisoners' work. Walk softly in the kitchen. Don't make my cake fall." Once, when I had rushed noisily into the kitchen letting the screen door bang behind me, I caused Mother's cake rising in the wood stove oven to collapse. It had been a cake for Sunday dinner; the preacher was coming. She took the cake out of the oven, dumped it into the slop bucket and told me, "Take this to the hogs now."

When I asked "Why now?" Mother said that there was no need to advertise a failure. "Feed it to the hogs, and no one need ever know." She had baked another.

ৡ◆৶

Approaching our house, the gravel road ran between my parents' hillside pasture on its east side and Mr. Mark Daves' bottomland on its west side. The prisoners' hard and hot work consisted of cutting the bushes and briars and thorny locust trees that were reaching out into the road from the steep bank up to Dad's pasture fence. As the prisoners worked their way toward our yard, I watched and listened to them wield their scythes, machetes, axes, and saws, trimming the thick growth all along the road on the high bank below our pasture fence.

At noon, sweating through their black and white striped uniforms, the men walked into the shade under the large maples of our yard. The ten prisoners laid their tools together near the roadside under one maple and spread out on the grass under the other shade trees. The guard, equally wet with sweat, leaned his rifle against another tree trunk and sat down in the shade, too.

The trustee opened the food chest and passed out sandwiches to the men. Then he refilled the water bucket with fresh, cold water from our well.

As the men ate, they often got up and took a drink from the tin cup kept hooked on the side of the water bucket. Before the prisoners finished their lunch, Mother sent me out with plates of cake and plates of pie, enough for every man, including the guard. After each ate his cake or pie, he rinsed his plate and fork at our pump and placed them on the edge of our kitchen porch with a "Thank you, ma'am" to my mother.

After they ate, the men rested and talked in the shade of our lawn until the guard told them, "Take up your tools."

Sleep Tight

It was during the Depression and before the beginning of World War II that Dad took an old rope bedstead from Grandfather and Grandmother Morgan's attic and set it up for me. Low to the floor, it had a headboard, small footboard, and side boards with holes in them for a rope to be woven back and forth as a support for the mattress, but there was no mattress.

For my bed, Dad removed the ropes and remade the side boards to hold slats, which he cut and laid crosswise as support for the tick Mother made to serve as my mattress. Dad told me, "When the ropes stretched, my bed became a hammock, and I had to tighten them."

No one in our home had a modern mattress when I was a small boy. I got my bed about the same time that Mother and Dad went to Asheville to a mattress factory for several days one month to make their own mattress. Until then my parents slept on a featherbed that they placed on top of their straw tick.

Dad said that "Sleep tight and don't let the bedbugs bite" originated far south where people filled their ticks with Spanish moss. Minute bugs crawl out of the moss and into the bedclothes of the sleeper's warm body.

ॐ ◆ ॐ

On a fall day when the leaves were paper dry, Mother took me and the new tick to the woods above our home. We went first to the grove of white pines where the ground under the trees was thick with clean, dry needles. I raked up the needles, and Mother stuffed them into the new, blue-striped, canvas-like tick. She also put in dry oak leaves, packing the tick tight-full. Back home, Mother sewed up the end of the tick with her needle and thread.

The years passed. Mother and Dad refilled my tick with straw early each fall. Sometimes a needle of straw or leaf stem would poke its way through the cloth of the tick and I would feel a pinprick. "My tick bit me," I told Mother.

Mother placed a washstand, also from my Morgan grandparents' attic, in my dormer. It was not a strictly private dormer as our home was not finished. During the Depression Dad could raise only eighty dollars to purchase material for our house. Powell Lumber Company of Canton told Dad that for two hundred dollars they could furnish material to complete the house with hardwood floors. The eighty dollars purchased enough lumber and doors and windows to build the house as far as it was structured in my childhood. The white, outside walls of German-styled siding, our home appeared to be finished, but inside we lived on the subfloors with only the living room and kitchen walls completed with wood. The dining room and downstairs bedroom were separated by the naked studding on which mother tacked cardboard from boxes on the studs to wall off each room. She also tacked cardboard against the outside wall studs for insulation.

The upstairs area where we all slept was spacious, open, with room for three large bedrooms including my dormer. Dad built a railing of wide boards around the stairwell opening in the center of the loft to prevent anyone's stepping over the edge and falling into the living room below. Mother hung curtains on wire lines to mark off the three areas as separate bedrooms. For closets we had cardboard wardrobes.

There was no ceiling material on the rafters above us nor any wallboard on the studding so we could see right up to the tin roofing that covered us and even out into the remote corners of the attic areas where the steep roof met the support walls of the house. The subfloor of the upstairs bedroom area was solid, but at night one could see light from below peeping through the cracks.

Cold air seeped through the cracks in winter. I awoke some mornings with powered snow on my top quilt. The twins and I would jump out of bed and take our clothes downstairs and dress in front of the open fireplace where Dad had a roaring fire. The fire pulled a draft of air from inside the house, so most of the heat went up the chimney. Getting dressed in winter in front of the fire became a kind of round dance as we turned to keep warm on all sides and not fall into the fire.

Mother took the clothes iron that Grandfather Anders made for her, heated it at the open fire, wrapped it in a towel and placed it at the foot of my bed to warm my feet. Also, she filled rubber bags with hot water and put them in my sisters' beds.

و⬥ى

I squirmed on my straw-filled mattress until I was deep in the tick, like a log floating on water, almost submerged. The tick around me was insulation against the cold of my dormer. With the warm iron at my feet and the heavy layers of homemade quilts over me with fresh, cool air to breathe, I could sleep tight.

A MIRACLE

"Joe, son, come here, please," Mother called me.

I looked up from the kitchen yard where my younger cousins and I were playing tag. Most of us were in our Sunday best as we had been to church that morning for Sunday School. The Southern Baptist quarterly lesson had been about the miracles of Christ: Jesus's feeding five thousand people with only one loaf of bread and two fishes and his turning water into wine at the wedding in Cana.

Dad and Mother had brought the twins and me as well as a cooker of chicken and dumplings to Grandmother Anders' home for Sunday dinner. It was an occasion to remember: Grandfather's birthday, August 26, 1874. My cousins came with their mothers. Three of Mother's brothers were in military service. Uncle Ray Anders, the youngest, was in the Army and already in England even before he started shaving; Uncle Glenn Anders was in the Army Air Force in the Pacific; Uncle Edgar Anders, Aunt Lean's husband, and Uncle Lloyd Little, Aunt Lura's husband, were in the Navy. It was 1942, and I was eight years old.

Mother waited at the kitchen door where she told me, "Run to the spring and bring the bucket of milk.

Dinner is about ready," As I turned to go, she added, "Be careful when you lift the lid on that old race. Don't drop the rock on the lid and break something."

I raced up the path between the beehives on my left and the spring stream on my right. On the other side of the stream, the clothesline stretched across the grass between the water's edge and the picket fence that surrounded the vegetable garden.

The open spring was a cool place even on that hot Sunday afternoon. Under the shade of the gum trees and the laurel bushes the pool was so clear the I could see the colors of the sand crystals and pebbles in the bottom of the spring. The water was much deeper than it appeared to be.

As I was hot from playing, it was too tempting not to unhook the gourd cup from the nail on the near tree and dip it into the spring and take a long drink. After hanging the gourd back on its hook, I turned to the milk race.

Grandfather had built the milk race years before he died. It was a long, strong, wood box that stood lengthwise over the stream of cold water that flowed under and through it, a natural refrigerator for any food that Grandmother needed to keep fresh and cool. It resembled a casket in its form and size. I lifted the rather heavy lid and leaned it against the back stay.

Inside, in the bottom of the race, there were flat rocks low in the water on which the food jars were placed. On the lid of each container there was a smooth, hand-size stone that held the containers steady in the stream and kept them from floating in the water.

I found a glass, gallon jar with milk in it, and removed its stone, and picked it up. It was rich whole milk from one of Grandmother's Jersey cows, but the jar was not even half full of milk. I began looking for more milk in other containers. There was a bucket of butter, a canister of cottage cheese, two jars of fresh cider, a jar of molasses, a dish of fresh peaches sitting on the shelf above water with other jars of food, but no bucket of milk. I closed the lid on the race.

When I put the milk jar on the sink counter in Grandmother's kitchen where all my aunts and grandmother were busy putting food on the table, I whispered to mother, "This is all the milk I found."

"Mama," Mother said quietly as she turned to Grandmother at the sink, "Is this all the milk you've got?"

"Yes. It'll be enough, Della," Grandmother said. Then she added, "Before Ray left for the Army, he traded his Jersey cow that was such a good milker to Fred Hall to cover all the bills I owed at the store."

"I should have thought," Mother said to me. "I could have brought a gallon of milk at least for all these children." We had been milking four cows at home and we had given milk to the hogs and poured the extra milk in the creek. We never poured milk on the ground because my mother believed that would "make the cows go dry."

I went back to join my cousins in the yard where even the smaller ones were making a game of jumping back and forth over the stream as it flowed over the yard. Grandfather had long ago placed a V-shaped trough under the water of the stream from the spring just above the large rock over which the water flowed before it crossed the kitchen yard. The knee-high waterfalls was about ten feet from the kitchen door.

Grandmother appeared and said, "Children, wash your hands there at the spout and come to the table." She handed me a towel, and added, "Joe, dry their hands for them."

ॐ ◆ ॐ

Memory of Grandfather was still very present in Grandmother's home. The long dining table, the chairs and the long bench accompanying it were made by him. Grandmother seated most us children on the bench that flanked the dining table lengthwise between the table and the dining area wall.

I was seated at the end of the bench near the kitchen part of the dining room. On the same bench and in the chairs at the other end of the table were my sisters, Dot and Dean; Aileen, Aunt Blanche's daughter; Tommy and Joan, Uncle Homer and Aunt Lean's two oldest; Jerry, Hal, and Clarence, Aunt Lura's oldest boys; and Billy, Earl, and Wade, Uncle Edgar and Aunt Katy's oldest boys. We sat very close together.

Father and Mother, then Uncle Homer and Aunt Lena with their one-year-old baby, Kenneth, and Aunt

Katy with one-year-old Earl sat on the other side of the table. Aunt Lura, with her one-year-old son Dan, Aunt Ruby, Aunt Belva, and Aunt Blanche took chairs in other parts of the kitchen. Grandmother took her place at the head of the table near me and asked my father, "Buddy, will you say grace?"

"Father, we thank you for this food," he began. "Bless it to the nourishment of our bodies and us to your service. Forgive us of our sins for Christ's sake. Amen." Until he was ninety, Dad always said that same blessing. However, while he was praying, I was counting the full glasses of milk at the plates of every one of my cousins. I glanced back at the glass jar of milk that stood on the sink counter. I could not believe that still had another pint or more of milk in it!

I looked at mother and at each of my aunts in turn. Each of those holding babies had milk in their bottles. No one seemed to notice that there was much more milk on the table than there was milk brought in from the spring race.

I thought of the miracles we had read about in Sunday School. I remembered that Grandmother had said, "It's enough," when I placed the jar on the sink counter, but I knew it was not enough milk to fill all those glasses and the bottles and have some left in the jar.

At home that evening I asked mother how the small amount of milk had become enough for everyone with some left over. Mother smiled and said, "The milk you brought was whole milk. Mama did what she often does. She added enough water to fill the milk jar up."

"She turned the water into milk!" I exclaimed. "That was a miracle!"

THE BUCKET OF COLD WATER

"Come here, Joe Dicky, and talk to me," Aunt Dixie called as I trudged across the lawn toward the well house. I was seven and I was the water boy for a field full of thirsty farm hands harvesting wheat in the hot June sun.

I was old enough to know, too, that Aunt Dixie was to be respected. Not really my aunt, she was the widow of Uncle Mont Jones, who originally owned this large farm. She was my Aunt Carrie's mother. Aunt Carrie and Uncle Oliver Morgan were childless.

My father was Uncle Oliver's youngest brother and one of many hands now in the wheat field.

I put the bucket down on the steps and stood at the edge of the porch. Aunt Dixie was in her eighties, a stately old woman seated in her cushioned rocking chair. She always wore a clean, long dress with an apron and a sweater on her shoulders. Today she had on a wide, white lace collar over a dark blue patterned dress, a special dress. She sat on the shaded end of the porch with a view of the hundred acres of bottomland before her.

"Mm-hmm," she began with her lips closed. "Tell me how they're a-doing this morning, Joe Dicky."

"Dad sent me for water," I replied.

"Yes, I see that, mm-hmm," she said. "They can wait. Who's down there a-helping?" She squinted her eyes and peered through the thick lenses of her gold-rimmed spectacles. "I see Marshall and Bud and your dad. Oliver's on the binder. Who's them others?"

I told her, "Uncle Gaston and Mr. Knight."

"Well, Amos is a good hand, mm-hmm," she said, referring to one of Uncle Oliver's tenants, Mr. Knight to me.

Of course, my father who was shocking wheat could see that I was standing on the porch but maybe he couldn't see Aunt Dixie behind the hedge bushes and the high banister. From a distance I heard my father shout, "Hey, JOOO, bring that water!"

Aunt Dixie motioned toward a chair. "Sit down, Joe Dicky," she said. "When Carrie comes she can send some gingerbread with the water." I didn't like gingerbread, but Aunt Carrie's hot out of the oven was an exception. Maybe Dad would forgive my delay if I brought a basket of gingerbread.

"Joe! Get the water!" Dad's insistent voice rang loud and clear from the valley. His motto for me was "quick as the word," but nobody left Aunt Dixie until he was dismissed. She was a bit deaf but surely she heard my father's voice.

She dipped snuff and had to spit. Her spittoon was on the floor. I handed her the copper tin with sand in the bottom. "Mm-hmm," she said, pursing her lips.

Only an expert could shoot a clean bubble of brown spittle from his lips into a nearby container without a tell-tale drip. Aunt Dixie held the tin on her thighs and aimed. Perhaps she was going to show this seven-year-old boy, whose practiced spittle aim was sure, how accurate an old lady could be.

Her mouth was quite full of the dark tobacco juice. She spit in a kind of spurt with the wad hitting the can, but then it became an elastic string of limp, brown phlegm that stretched from tin to chin over her white lace collar and clean print dress.

I watched as she reached for a linen handkerchief that Aunt Carrie had placed close on her side table. Carefully and silently Aunt Dixie wiped at her dress front. Finally, she put her handkerchief down and breathed "mm-hmm."

"Look at me, Joe Dicky. Take a good look. You use tobacco and you'll look like this someday." After a quiet pause, she added her "mm-hmm."

It wasn't the bucket of cold water nor the basket of fresh ginger cake that saved me from the sharp words of my impatient father. It was Uncle Oliver who said, "Don't be cross with the boy, Buddy. Carrie's made him wait for the bread."

UNDER THE BLAZING SUN

Dad and I were in the woodyard splitting stove wood. When I turned from the chopping block to select another log section, I saw Mr. Parks shuffling his way along the road toward us. It wasn't the first time the elderly man had trudged up to our house under a blazing sun, wearing his heavy wool Army-surplus coat.

While I continued to split wood, I remembered a day years before when I must have been a tow-headed boy, bare-footed and shirtless in short dungarees. I had run to meet Mr. Parks where he paused and watched my approach. With me beside him, he had shuffled one foot in front of the other out of the road and toward our kitchen porch. The porch floor was about two feet above the yard and without railing or bannister, so Mr. Parks, as I was required to address him, sat down on the edge of the porch floor with his feet on the yard. It was a welcome place to sit out of the sun.

Mr. Parks had come at noon and Dad had insisted he "sit a spell and have a bite to eat with us." Mother set an extra plate on the table, and she sent me to the garden for more tomatoes.

Dad and Mother always welcomed people who walked the road by our home. Dad said, "You never know who you might be helping or have as a visitor. Remember that story in the Bible about Abraham and Lot? They entertained angels but didn't know it." He also mentioned that Jesus had said, "As oft as ye do it unto the least of these, ye do it also unto me."

I remembered one evening when two men arrived late at our door and asked for permission to sleep in the loft on the hay in our cow barn. Dad had said, "Why sure, just don't smoke in the barn." He added, "You'll like the smell of the fresh alfalfa and don't mind the cats. They keep the mice down. The black snake helps the cats with the mice."

Mother fixed each man a dish of food from our table and told them to help themselves at the well and at the grapevines. She added, "Fill your pockets with apples and plums in the morning before you leave."

Dad had told me that when he was a boy, a blind man came walking in one day led by his seeing-eye dog, and asked Grandfather Morgan if he could spend the night. Dad never forgot that when Grandmother Morgan told my father to catch a chicken to fry for dinner, the blind man had said, "Take my dog with you and point at the chicken you want to catch, and my dog will catch it for you." The dog did. Also the blind man could identify each piece of currency and even the denomination of paper money by feeling each bill or coin. He had taught Dad how to do it, too.

"If you listen to strangers and travelers," Dad told me, "you can always learn things from them."

❧◆❧

On that day years before, when I was a tow-headed boy, Mr. Parks wore his long heavy wool winter coat over a wool suit, dark shirt, and tie. A broad-brimmed felt hat shaded his eyes. Discussion of Mr. Parks' clothes was forbidden in his presence, but the question that hung constantly on my lips was, "Mr. Parks, why do you wear that coat in the summertime?"

With his eyes, Dad had let me know not to be impolite and ask what I had on my mind. "It's Mr. Parks' business what he wears," Dad had always said, and he had added, "I don't understand how the old man could bear the heat in that suit and coat, but let well-enough alone."

At table Mr. Parks had eaten slowly and enough for two meals—green beans simmered all morning in pork fat, hot buttered cornbread, hot corn on the cob boiled and salted and buttered, okra fried in corn meal, sweet pickles, sliced sweet onions, cold sliced tomatoes, mashed potatoes washed down with cold sweet tea. He had even accepted a piece of pie and a piece of Mother's walnut cake.

After Dad excused himself and went back to the field, Mr. Parks had declared he "must mosey on over the mountain." He was going to visit with his sister on South Turkey Creek.

I walked along beside the old man a short way up

the road before I did the forbidden. "Mr. Parks, why do you wear that coat in the summertime?"

He stopped and looked down at me. "Whatever keeps out cold, can keep out heat."

On that late August day, after accepting a drink of cold water from our well, Mr. Parks left our wood-yard. Before Dad and I returned to splitting wood, we watched the old man plod on up the road under the blazing sun and his heavy wool coat.

41

PART THREE

THE WHIP SPOKE

There'll never be another Lee Hamlet," Aunt Bess said when she heard that he'd been killed.

It was on an early damp, foggy November morning that I first met Lee. I heard him before I saw him. It was so foggy that nothing was visible more than thirty feet away. I stood in a circle of gray light.

Suddenly, I heard three cracks like distant rifle shots muffled in the morning mist. Then into the privacy of my thoughts I heard, "Hii! Yii! Wheee! Step it up, Hell hounds! Step it up! Fair is foul and foul is fair. Hover through the fog and filthy air." It was a clear, powerful voice that cut through the valley. Then again came three sharp cracks.

I left the pen where I was watching and listening to the fattening hogs slurp their slop and ran into the barn where Dad was feeding the cattle. I looked in at Dad; we listened together a moment to the approaching infernal shouts and the snapping of a mean whip.

"That's Lee Hamlet coming to do the logging for your Uncle Oliver," Dad answered my silent question. I had heard stories of Lee Hamlet, how he had spent time in prison, how he had escaped and was caught and then served out his time. "Paid his debt to society," Dad had said. Also I had heard he was the toughest mountain man who ever lived. He was afraid of nothing.

It was said that at some Baptist revival meeting, Deacon Doc Gaddy had gone to Lee during the altar call and had asked the young man, "Son, don't you want to go to heaven?" to which Lee had answered, "No."

"Then go to hell," Mr. Gaddy had quipped and returned to his pew. Lee was not known to be a religious man.

ॐ ♦ ॐ

I stood under the dogwood tree at the corner of the barn staring into the fog, waiting. Then below me on the gravel road, like an apparition, the heads of two plodding oxen formed out of the mist. I discerned their yoke, then both huge beasts. Finally, Lee appeared some little distance behind the team, cracking his long black-snake whip at intervals.

"Hey, Lee!" my Dad shouted at him as the oxen plodded along below our barn, "come to breakfast!"

"Whoa!" Lee commanded his oxen. The yoked team stopped still. "I had breakfast long ago, Buddy. Thanks just the same," Lee told my father.

I ran through the barn, scrambled down the bank and under the grapevines to get a better look at the oxen. They were Red Devons each weighing over fifteen hundred pounds, as large as Uncle Oliver's great Hereford bull, but they were all one color, no white spots or shades of red, just a dark, yellowish red in the morning light. Their horns, gleaming like polished black and white marble, grew forward, then dipped into curves that turned upward and pointed ahead.

I learned later that Lee had selected them as calves, castrated them himself, fed and trained them as draft animals. Devons, bred in Devonshire, England, had been used as draft animals many years before shorthorn cattle were developed and before Devons came to be bred for beef.

I found myself looking up to these oxen as I walked around the team. Each stood quietly, with half-closed eyes as if he wanted to catch up on his sleep as Lee and my father talked. The large yoke rested across their shoulders. Lee had made it himself.

"That's the third damned yoke I've fit on these devils," Lee remarked as I regarded it. "I make 'em to fit the size of the oxen and my needs," he added.

"What kind of wood is that?" I asked.

"Yellow poplar, boy," he quipped. "Best wood for yokes, but my bows around under their necks are hickory. It bends without breaking."

The yoke, hewn from one round piece, curved gently over the broad shoulders of each ox, the bows a loose necklace that didn't encumber their breathing. From the thick center of the yoke, a large iron ring hung from a spike. A huge logging chain attached to the ring dragged between the oxen and trailed on behind them. There were no reins, only the whip Lee held curled in his right hand. The oxen were driven by Lee's voice, and his whip just punctuated his commands.

The blacksnake whip Lee had made from rawhide.
The long, wood handle worn slick by his grip extended
into the platted leather strips that were woven round
and extended at least ten feet to a single, limber, leather
string that would raise a blister if it touched flesh.

So accurate with his whip, Lee Hamlet could kill a
fly on one of his oxen and not harm a hair. He could kill
a snake with it ten feet away, and he said he often killed
snakes that way. "They come not between the dragon
and his wrath," he added. However, the oxen bore no
marks of Lee's whip on their hides. The whip spoke to
them as it cracked around their ears.

"How about you knocking my dogs out of the logs
when these critters pull 'em down in the yard ?" Lee
asked me. (Dogs is the logger's term for the sharp spikes
driven into the end of the log and then connected to
the pull chain.)

"Sure," I told him.

"Well, stand back," he advised me as he hurled his
whip and cracked it just above the oxen's heads. "Mac-
Beth! Banquo! Ho!" he shouted. The oxen leaned forward and moved on up the gravel with a lively step, the
heavy logging chain and dogs dragging between them,
Lee following behind.

I stood watching them fade from sight into the fog,
but Lee kept up his bright talk to his team, "Pillicock
sat on Pillicock Hill. Alow! Alow! Aloooow!" He never
called the oxen by the same name twice. His voice rang
in the valley. As I watched him disappear into the mist,

I knew it would be a wonder to watch him and listen to his talk all day.

೪◆ల

After chores were finished, I set out for Uncle Oliver's log yard. Along the road I met Uncle Gaston Cole standing at Aunt Bess and Uncle Taylor's mailbox waiting for the postman's Mercury to bring the *Asheville Citizen.*

"Uncle Gaston," I asked, "did you see Mr. Lee Hamlet and his oxen go up the road this morning?"

"No, I didn't see him, but surely everybody on Newfound heard him," he said flatly.

"I like to hear him talk to his oxen," I said.

"You could listen to someone more erudite and edifying," he mumbled. "Lee Hamlet never had any education to speak of, too obstreperous to study." My great- uncle did not share my enthusiasm. He continued, "Lee attended that little school years ago but he was no scholar."

I knew that Uncle Gaston had gone to college and that he read magazines and the daily newspaper and his Bible every Sunday morning on the porch while Aunt Bess and Uncle Taylor went to Zion Hill Baptist Church. He was very learned.

I said, "I'm going to help log today. I'm going to knock the dogs out of the logs for Lee when the oxen pull them down into the yard."

"You'll not learn anything useful listening to that man curse those poor animals," Uncle Gaston told me.

It was very clear that Uncle Gaston did not admire Lee Hamlet, but then Uncle Gaston was not a logger, and I was sure he couldn't handle a mule, much less a team of oxen.

Aunt Bess was in the garden nearby and she called out to me, "Joe Dicky, tell Lee to come down here for dinner. You come, too."

I left Uncle Gaston standing at the mailbox watching the mountain road for the Mercury, and I hurried on to Uncle Oliver's yard, knowing it would be exciting to work with and listen to this marvelous man.

ço ◆ ớ

By midmorning the mist had disappeared, revealing a cool, sky-blue day. I hung around Aunt Carrie, ready to run to the log yard and knock out the dogs from the logs when the oxen dragged them down the logging trail to the log yard. I heard Lee directing his team near the mountaintop. "Draw! You rascals, draw!" The whip cracked. From the foot of the logging trail, I could hear him discussing things with the Devons even though he and the oxen were at least five hundred feet in elevation and distance above me up the mountain.

"Stand! You boiled-brained baggage!"

"Be idle-headed, motley-minded a minute!" I heard him hammer in the dogs.

"Gee! I said gee! Now pull, you rogues and peasant slaves! Pull!" The whip cracked.

I couldn't see the oxen, but I knew that they were heading down the road with two large logs trailing behind them, one behind the other. Lee appeared out on the ridge from which he could see and direct the Devons lumbering down the trail toward me.

"Steady! You dizzy-eyed clay-brains!" The whip cracks echoed in the hills.

The logging trail followed beside an almost dry stream that flowed in the gulch between the two ridges. Punctuating his commands with the crack of his whip, Lee kept up his incessant commands from the ridge as the oxen followed the wide, well-worn trail.

"Flap dragon! Haw! Haw!' A crack of the whip.

"Horn-beast! Hugger-mugger!" Crack.

"Nero! Fiddle! Fiddle!"

The oxen came steadily down the trail pulling wide at curves. As the logs rolled against those already in the yard, I shouted "Whoa!" The bovines stopped. After knocking the dogs from the logs with the go-devil, I yelled "Ready" to Lee who waited on the ridge.

"Stand in front of the be-slubbering beasts," Lee directed me. I ran around in front of the team and waved my arms for them to go back up the ravine trail.

"Haw! Haw! You lumpish loggerheads, Haw!" The oxen slowly turned together under their heavy yoke.

"Hii! Hii whee!" from the ridge. The great Devons stepped lively as they climbed back up the trail, the heavy log chain and dogs sliding snakelike between and behind them. I sat on a log and listened to Lee and waited for the oxen to return dragging more logs.

ço◆ལ

I knew that Aunt Bess had taught school in a one-room schoolhouse on Turkey Creek before she married Uncle Taylor, so while she placed the last of the dinner on the table and before Lee or Uncle Gaston appeared in the dining room, I said, "Uncle Gaston said Lee was 'obstress something' when he was young. What does that mean?"

"Obstreperous?" she asked.

"Yes."

"Oh! Noisy. Boisterous. Your great-uncle always uses a fifty-cent word when a five-cent word would do just as well."

After Lee and I were seated at the dinner table and Aunt Bess sat down, she said, "Let's eat while the food is warm. Your Uncle Gaston will come when he gets washed up."

I supposed that Uncle Gaston had read the morning paper from cover to cover and then had split some stove wood at the shed that morning. Certainly he had not helped Aunt Bess in the garden. Uncle Taylor was working at the Morgan Furniture Factory in Asheville.

I listened to Lee and Aunt Bess talk about crops and family, and we were about finished with dinner and ready for cake and ice cream when Uncle Gaston appeared and took his place.

He sat down and then took out his pocketknife and began to clean each fingernail and wipe the blade on his trouser leg. Finally, when he appeared ready to eat, Aunt Bess passed him a dish of fried chicken.

"Bessie, reckon this fried food won't upset my stomach?" he asked her. Aunt Bess coaxed him into trying some of everything, and I noted that he ate with relish and didn't seem to be any closer to death. We left Uncle Gaston still eating at the table.

"Thanks, Bess, for the good dinner," Lee said. "I'd better exercise my beef-witted bovines before Oliver thinks I'm loafing. You and Taylor come down and visit some day. Bring that girl of yours and this boy along. I believe he'll make a good logger."

ॐ ♦ ॐ

Years later, Lee's death was sudden. On July 11, 1957, he was loading logs onto a truck when one of the skid poles broke under the weight of the last log. It dropped onto Lee, crushing him against the earth. Preacher Howard Mann, his only helper that day, witnessed the accident.

ॐ ♦ ॐ

Wiping tears from his eyes, my father said, "There's no telling how much lumber he's logged out of these mountains. Everybody thought a lot of Lee."

"Yes," Aunt Bess agreed, "there'll never be another Lee Hamlet."

The Witch and the Well

"You can drink from that well, but not the cows, if you want to sell Grade A milk," Lee Hollers, the health inspector, told my Uncle Taylor. Riley Palmer, the county farm agent, had brought the inspector with him to the farm. The farm agent and I glanced from Dad to Aunt Bess to Uncle Taylor and back to the inspector. Aunt Bess and Dad never took their eyes off him. He was referring to the well at the home were they and their ten siblings had been born and grew into healthy adults, where Grandfather and Grandmother Morgan had lived the best part of their eighty plus years, where I and my generation of cousins loved to play and stay, and where Aunt Bess and Uncle Taylor now lived.

There were two wells on the farm—one at the house that had always been hard water and one at the horse barn that had always been soft water. They were on the two sides of the main creek that flowed through the farm. My grandmother Morgan and my six aunts had discovered years before I was born that water drawn from the well at the horse barn was best for washing hair.

Agent Palmer explained, "Your well at the house is too susceptible to contamination, especially surface water. Your kitchen sink-drain flows along beside the house toward the wash house near the well. To sell Grade-A milk, the health department requires that milk cows drink water from a source free of any possibility of bacteria. Mr. Hollers must regularly test the water you use in the dairy barn."

Uncle Taylor's new barn and cow lot replaced all the vegetable garden area that had been on the side of the creek nearer the house. The new modern, cinder-block dairy had a milking parlor for six cows complete with individual drinking cups, a feed storage room that opened conveniently to the row of mangers, and a clinically clean milk room where cans filled with milk were kept cool in the large refrigeration unit. All milk containers and utensils were scalded twice a day, and the milk room kept disinfected by soap and very hot water. The lounging barn and the silo were nearing completion on the pasture side of the dairy. The old plank dairy barn across the creek and above the hog pens and the chicken house was given over to new-born calves.

However, Mr. Riley Palmer and Mr. Lee Hollers were talking about the need for a third well on the farm. Suddenly, Mr. Palmer asked, "By-the-way, Mr. Sluder, you gave me three samples of water to test: one from the horse barn well, which is good water; one from the house well, which we suspect; and a sample you also wanted tested. Where did you get it?"

"How did it test?" Uncle Taylor asked.

"Pure. It is cleaner than Asheville's drinking water."

"I got it out of the branch where the cows drink. It flows from the mountain yonder, through the center of the pasture." Lee Hollers raised an eyebrow as he looked beyond the dairy to the water flowing between him and the cherry orchard. "You have nothing to worry about there. However," he added, "to be on the safe side, you need to have another well just for the dairy."

ೋ♦ৎ

Because Uncle Taylor was employed full time at the Morgan Furniture Factory in Asheville, he left it up to Dad to get Mr. Buford Garner, the water diviner, to locate the best place to dig the well for the dairy. Mr. Garner was a short, friendly, open man of about seventy who had a Santa Claus stomach and smiled easily.

Since dowsers who found water for mountain wells were often called water witches, I had expected someone out of the ordinary. Dad had told me of one Noah Buckley, a water witch, who wore a rattlesnake skin belt to prevent getting rheumatism. "But," Dad said, "it was his power to find good water that made Mr. Buckley famous." Dad said that Noah Buckley used only peach tree twigs for his water wand. When he walked about holding a prong in each hand, he mumbled, "Water, water, if you be there, bend this twig and show me where." When his water wand twig bent low to the earth it was always a good place to dig a well."

ೋ♦ৎ

Before the elderly Mr. Buford Garner got out of his truck, Dad instructed me, "Just watch and listen.

Don't distract Buford when he's working." However, Mr. Garner was a talker who shared his ideas freely. He arrived in the late morning, and he didn't go to work right away. He and Dad and Aunt Bess sat down in the yard chairs and talked about the new dairy and the need for the well to be close to the dairy barn.

"They's water underground ever wher," Mr. Garner said, "but to get a well with plenty of good water, you need to dig into a underground stream. If they's a underground stream close to the barn, I'll find it.

"Most dowsers use a green, peach-tree fork," Mr. Garner told us. "Some use a probing wire. That's a copper wire. I know of a man in Georgia who uses any Y shaped twig as long as it's green and pliable. He puts the end of one prong into his teeth and the end of the other prong against his thumb. With one prong in his teeth and one against his thumb, he can't begin to control the twig. The dowser don't control the wand. It has to be free."

"Does he find water?" I asked.

"Oh, yes!" Mr. Garner looked at me. "He's found hundreds o' wells in Georgia."

☙ ◆ ❧

Mr. Garner surveyed the field above the barn that rose to the beginning of the mountain pasture. He explained that there was probably a stream of water running underground down toward the creek. "It might be the vein that feeds yore house well." He walked up the hillside above the dairy barn.

Dad, Aunt Bess, and I watched as he took up his peach-tree fork, one prong in each hand, holding it with his thumbs outside and the twig held waist high, parallel to the ground. He walked up the ridge of the clear field above the dairy toward the mountain pasture and then began to walk back and forth across an imagined possible source of water that might be flowing down toward the house. He walked very slowly. Whenever his twig dipped of its own accord, he stopped and marked the place with a small rock. We watched in silence. Soon it became clear that the rocks he placed formed a line down the slope.

When Mr. Garner reached the lower edge of the field close to a tall maple tree, he told Dad and Aunt Bess, "The wand says they's a vein o' water runnin' under here towards the house. It might be the same vein o' water that feeds yore well at the house. Dig here and you'll have plenty o' water."

He looked at the tree and said, "This maple likely drinks from this vein. The only trouble with a well here is the roots o' this maple may get in the well. Maples do that you know." He stuck the fork end of his wand into the ground and said, "If the water at the house gets muddy when you dig here, you'll know that you've dug into the same vein."

After the place to dig the well was decided, Aunt Bess said, "Buford, dinner's ready, so come on in and eat before you go."

As we were eating, I asked, "Mr. Garner, why do people call you a water witch?"

He smiled across the table at me, swallowed a sip of ice tea and said, "I'm also called a diviner." He was silent a moment before he added, "Dowsing is an art, not a science. Nobody knows why divinin' rods work. Some folks believe it's magic. That might explain being called a witch." He rested a moment, looked me in the eyes, and then said, "When my dowsing rod is pulled downward by some unknown force, I knows they's just more things in heaven and earth than we can explain."

After dinner, Mr. Garner said, "I must be gettin' along."

"Buford, what do we owe you?" Dad asked.

"I don't never charge for dowsing," Mr. Garner snapped. "It's a gift from the Good Lord. Some people give me a few dollars after they've dug their well. I give it to the church. I don't do this to make money."

"We're much obliged," my father said. The men shook hands before the old man climbed into his truck.

ॐ ◆ ॐ

The well diggers dug about ten feet down in that spot and struck clear water. They dug another five feet just to get a good water basin, and we had all the water we needed for the dairy. The health department promoted our dairy milk from Grade C to Grade A. In the pasture the cows continued to drink from the mountain stream.

THE REAL THING

"He's your horse," Dad told me as I admired the young stallion in the barn lot. "You need to get acquainted with him. You can feed him every morning and evening, before and after school." Listening to Dad, I stood with my mouth open and my eyes fixed on the horse.

"He's not a year old yet," Dad talked on while I watched and listened. "He's not broke. We can train him as a riding horse and break him to team with Tom or Kate."

"Dad, he's beautiful. What kind of horse is he?"

"Tennessee Walker."

"Does he just walk?" I wanted a horse that I could ride like the cowboys in the movies.

"Oh, he can run. He's bred for saddle and work. I've been watchin' for just such a horse."

Dad took me to the Paramount when we were in Asheville to see Roy Rogers or Gene Autry in a black-and-white film. As I got my eyes adjusted to the bright sunlight after we were outside the theater, and while I was still under the enchantment of the cowboys or a lone western ranger, I told Dad, "If I had a horse I could ride him to get the cows."

Dad would say, "Yea," never promising anything.

As we stood in the passage at the barn, a man stopped his truck near the plank fence and called, "What kinda' horse is that?"

"A Tennessee Walker. Part Pacer. Part American Saddle. Part Morgan."

"Is he for sale?"

"Not today," Dad grinned and turned back to me. The horseman drove away.

"Morgan horse! He'll be part of the family," I exclaimed, but Dad ignored my remark.

"The Tennessee Walker is even tempered. He can learn to turn a row without stomping on plants."

"Can I work him?"

"When we break him and train him." I felt very lucky. "Look at his powerful neck and shoulders. How sleek and muscular. Strong legs. He'll make a good match for Tom."

"I like his white feet and that blaze of white on his face." I couldn't take my eyes off him.

"You want to call him White Feet?" Dad asked.

"How about Blaze?"

"Blaze. Maybe." Dad said. "He's a show horse."

"Really?"

"And he's world-renowned for his four-beat gait."

"What's that?"

"It's a gait that no other breed of horse has been able to learn. The way he walks and trots is said to be the most comfortable horse ride in the world."

61

ɷ✦ɷ

In the short weeks that followed, I thought of Blaze as more a pony than a stallion. He had been led by his halter when he was delivered to the farm, and he seemed to like his stall. Grandfather Morgan's horse barn was built with four large horse stalls, each of which opened onto a wide central hallway, or passage, on the ground level where the mules and Blaze were curried and harnessed. Three stalls and the stairwell to the great drive-in hayloft above were on the northeast end of the barn. On the southwest side of the central grooming hallway, Grandfather placed the other stores of the barn: the corn crib, the big feed and tack room, the fourth stall, a machine equipment shed, and a long cattle barn area with a feeding manger that stretched the width of the barn. Blaze had the best horse home in Newfound Valley.

Blaze was not the first farm animal that Dad gave me. Besides my dogs, which had been strays left by Asheville people on Sunday drives in the country, there had been a bull calf born on my seventh birthday to Old Roan, our best milk cow. Dad had said, "This calf can be yours, if you wean him and teach him to drink from a bucket. He can run with the beef cattle for the summer, and I'll sell him for veal in the fall. You can keep the money." I called him March.

For the first three days of his life March nursed Old Roan. Then Mother helped me wean him. She poured some milk into a small bucket. "He's hungry," she began. "Set the bucket on the straw, dip one hand into the bucket and then let the calf suck the milk from your fingers. Keep dipping your fingers into the milk and letting him suck 'em."

When March tasted the milk on my fingers, I began to hold my hand in the milk while March sucked my fingers. In his hunger and haste, he butted my hand and fingers in the bucket just as if it were his dam's udder. In no time he got the idea, and I just held the bucket for him as he drank the milk. That little bullock was my first bovine.

By the time I was ten, I was a regular milker at the dairy where I was beginning to build my own herd of cows. By the time I was thirteen, Dad woke me at 4:30 every morning and I went to the dairy to milk the eight cows that were my duty. After cleaning up at the dairy I ran home, changed clothes and caught the school bus by seven o'clock. Milking the cows started all over again every evening.

Nevertheless, I had many days to work with Blaze. He loved to run. It was wonderful to see him race around the barn lot with the mules after they were unharnessed and released from work. The mules, however, never got seriously into the race. As Blaze was growing fast and needed to be out of the barn, Dad let him pasture with the beef cattle much of that summer.

Mother gave me sugar cubes to keep in my pockets, and when I walked in the pasture where Blaze was, he came to me and took the cubes from my hand.

"I'll need a saddle," I told Dad one day.

"Ask your Uncle Oliver if he'll give you one of his saddles," Dad said. "There are two or three saddles up there hanging in that smokehouse." Dad looked away toward Uncle Oliver's place. "Years ago your aunt and uncle used to ride together." Dad was silent a moment and then said, "Your uncle might still have that old McClellan saddle that Uncle Mont Jones brought back from the Civil War."

Ɂ♦ɂ

When I saw the saddles, there was only one that I wanted. Uncle Oliver showed me the sidesaddle that Aunt Carrie had used back when women wore long dresses and never sat straddle the horse. Then Uncle Oliver pointed to the one I wanted on the wall hooks. It was black leather, without a horn on it like the ones that I had seen in the movies. It was definitely not a fancy Western saddle made for roping cows from horseback, but even while it was covered with dust and a few cobwebs, it was to me the most beautiful, smooth, black leather saddle I had ever seen.

As he took the saddle down from the wall, Uncle Oliver explained, "This is an English riding saddle. Sometimes it is called a flat saddle because it has almost no pommel or cantle."

"What is a pommel or cantle?"

"The pommel is the upper part of the saddle or the knob in the front." Uncle Oliver put his hand on the pommel. "The cantle is the rear part of the seat, which in that McClellan would give the rider a bit of back rest." He pointed to a saddle on the wall. "This is a good saddle for you and your yearling." I knew that a yearling was a one-year-old horse.

Uncle Oliver laid the saddle on the table there in the smokehouse and took a sack and wiped the dust and cobwebs off it. "You won't need a pad under this saddle because it is well padded." He said as he cleaned the leather. I didn't have a pad so that was good news, but Uncle Oliver asked, "Does Blaze have high withers?"

"I don't know," I told him. "What are withers?"

Uncle Oliver laughed and then told me, "The withers is your horse's highest constant point, the prominent ridge where the neck and back join. The height of a horse is measured vertically from the ground to the withers." I realized I had a lot to learn about horses.

Uncle Oliver continued, "These flaps are set well to the front—sometimes horsemen call then fenders—because this saddle is ridden with the riders's weight forward, over the horse's center of gravity. These flaps will keep your trousers from rubbing the sweat from the horse."

"The stirrups may be short for me," I commented.

"You can adjust them, but this saddle is ridden with stirrups shorter than a regular saddle."

My saddle had just plain metal stirrups and a wide band of leather for the clinch. There were no strings or carved leather or silver work as I had imagined I would like. When I later looked at fancy saddles and their price tags that ran as high as ten thousand dollars, I had a new appreciation of Uncle Oliver's gift.

When I brought my saddle into the barn where we kept Blaze, Dad said, "Your uncle never had a son to use that saddle. Take good care of it. Rub neat's foot oil into it every few days to soften up the leather."

However, I was never to ride Blaze in that saddle.

Because I was engaged at the dairy barn both morning and evening every day of the year, it was Dad who came to feed and train Blaze. He had always fed the livestock, and he took special interest in training Blaze. That summer, after I finished washing up at the dairy and got to the horse barn, Dad would have already fed and watered the horse and the mules. While Blaze was hitched to his chain in the passage outside his stall, I curried and brushed him. Dad and I talked as we worked.

Dad had made a bridle for Blaze out of old bridles and leather in the tack room, and he had fitted it to Blaze. At first Blaze was reluctant to take the bit, but Dad was patient. He used a snaffle bit, which is a jointed bit with two large rings to keep the bit from being pulled through the horse's mouth. "It might be wise to start with a curb bit," Dad mused, "in case he learns to take the bit in his teeth and go as he pleases like Tom did."

Tom was a parrot-mouthed mule (Dad called it a "Monkey Mouth") who would take a snaffle bit in his teeth and just walk away when he pleased. To keep him under control, Dad had the blacksmith make a double bit with joints that Tom could not ignore.

As Dad helped me make a harness for Blaze out of leather and material in the tack room, he talked about training horses. "A horse by nature is a grazing animal," Dad said. "Horses are fleet-footed herbivores—like deer, antelopes, and such. In the wild, their safety depends on their heels. Like all herbivores, horses are naturally apprehensive. Some are high-strung and are constantly tense and nervous like Kate, your Uncle Taylor's mule. The quietest horse, though, is still suspicious of anything strange. A sudden move or noise will startle him. If he can't run, he'll kick."

Dad had told me the same things about mules; nevertheless he was taking no chances with me. I knew the inborn apprehensiveness of horses and mules is the root of most of the troubles that plague horsemen. Dad warned me that horses, like mules, have little reasoning ability, but that they have long memories. "A horse is a creature of habit," he taught me.

Dad warned me, "Blaze will remember bad habits just like he remembers good habits, and it's not easy for him to forget bad habits. You must do his thinking for him."

My father had a lifetime of working with mules and horses. He cautioned me to be more patient and understanding than my horse could be. "He's a stallion, but don't ever forget that he has the same small brain as any other horse. Don't whip him or shout at him for not doing what you expect. It will only confuse him, and it can turn him into a nervous wreck."

"Do you think Blaze has ever been whipped?" I asked Dad.

"We'll never know. I don't think so, but it's the way we train him that matters."

"We can train him to be devoted to us."

"No, Son," Dad was quick to correct me. "This horse is not a creature of intelligence or devotion in a storybook. Blaze is the real thing."

I let Blaze watch when we put the harness on the mules, and then after I curried him, I brought the saddle to him and let him see and smell it before laying it on his back. He turned a wild eye at me, and when the saddle was on his back, he stomped around a bit and shook it off. Finally, Dad stood on the other side of the horse and passed the strap to me underneath, and I buckled it tight. When he got used to having the saddle strapped on him, I led him around the barn. We did the same with the harness so he could get used to wearing it. Dad said, "We can work him with Tom before you try to ride him."

It was soon apparent that Blaze was growing into a stallion. When he got sight of Mr. Mark's horses in their field, Blaze would whinny at them. When teamed with Tom who was larger than he and who was a very quiet and calm mule, Blaze got the hang of team work. For several weeks, Dad teamed Blaze only with Tom.

Blaze quickly became a picture of good health and beauty, but he was much more delicate and expensive to keep than a mule. When Blaze allowed me to hold up each of his hooves in turn while Dad cleaned and trimmed them, I rewarded him with a lump of sugar. Dad told me, "You need to get a farrier to make him some shoes, and you need to get the vet to geld him. It'll be expensive. Blaze will have to be castrated if we keep him as a draft animal."

I began to understand that training and caring for Blaze added hazard and danger as well as extra expense to my full schedule of school and farm work. Winter or summer, my work day began before sun-up and it ended after the last cow was milked and fed and the barn cleaned. Summer passed very quickly that year.

It had been a beautiful Indian Summer day, when I got off the school bus and headed for the horse barn. I found Dad coming out of the feed and tack room. He looked at me.

"Can I take Blaze out for a walk?" I asked.

"Not right now," Dad said with firmness.

"Something wrong?"

"Blaze and Kate ran away this afternoon. I just now got Blaze quieted down and in his stall."

"Really? Where? Is he OK?"

"No. He's not hurt. Kate's not either." I watched Dad's face and listened. "They tore up their harnesses. You can look at 'em later in the tack room."

"Where did it happen?"

"In the orchard. I hate it that they got away from me. I was just gathering some apples. I had the sledge. I thought it such an easy job that I would team Blaze with Kate. That was my mistake. I had no one to hold the reins while I picked up some apples." Dad wiped at his face with his red bandanna. He was a bit shaky.

"I dropped a sack of apples on the sledge. Blaze shied against Kate, she jerked forward, and they were off. I grabbed for the reins but they were too fast for me. They ran down the orchard towards the barn, apples spilling everywhere. Kate went on one side of a tree and Blaze went on the other. That's what stopped 'em."

That night after supper, Dad asked me, "Do you think you ought to sell Blaze?" I was expecting the question. Dad had given me my dream stallion, and he had let me taste the responsibility that came with him. Blaze was the real thing.

∻♦∻

When I joined the Marines during the Korean War and left the farm, my saddle was still hanging in the tack room collecting dust and cobwebs.

STOPPED IN HIS TRACKS

"I'll ax Oliver," Jim said to me as I stopped the mules near the barn. It was Jim's response to my question "Where should we unload this wagon?"

Jim Dills was one of four sons of Garland Dills, tenant farmer for Uncle Oliver Morgan. There was Sam, Bobby, and John Henry, his brothers all working in the fields with their father, my father, and some hired men. Uncle Oliver was walking toward us from his house.

Being a smart aleck, I teased Jim, "You don't really mean to ax my uncle, do you? What's he done to you?"

Jim glanced at me, then he looked down at the load of corn before he said quietly, "No, you're vexing me." I realized in that moment that I had not only hurt his feelings, but as his friend I was a disappointment. I was making fun of his pronunciation.

After Uncle Oliver told us where to unload the corn, Jim and I worked in silence. The Dills family were new tenant farmers for my uncle, and I could not have been happier to have four young men around my age for company. Sam was soon to enlist in the Navy and leave us before I got to know him well. Jim was my age and attended school with me in my class. Bobby was two years younger and John Henry was four years younger than Jim. After evening chores, we all played softball in our yard until our parents called us in at dark.

That evening after Dad and I finished the milking at the dairy barn, fed the mules at the horse barn, put out hay for the beef cattle in the lot, and started walking down the road toward home, I told Dad about what Jim and I had said to each other.

Dad stopped in his tracks right there in the road and looked at me. He held me with his eyes. I felt his disappointment in me as I had felt Jim's.

"Jim also says *hit* for *it* and he says *ain't* all the time, too." I asserted. "Mrs. Medlin says that *ain't* is a contraction for *am not* and should not be used as a contraction for *is not* or *are not*. We should speak the King's English.

"Mrs. Medlin said that one ought not to use *ain't* at all because when a Yankee hears you use it, he won't know whether you're using it correctly or not. Yankees will think you're illiterate." Dad watched me fidget.

"I was just teasing him," I defended myself.

"You understood what he meant, didn't you?" Dad asked me.

"Yes."

Dad held me with his eyes and said patiently, "Son, a little learning is a dangerous thing. You're not the standard for speaking English, nor is anyone else in this country. You sound like an old maid schoolmarm who has a bookish knowledge of the world and not enough knowledge of the heart. Communication is hard enough in this world without correcting or teasing another person when you know what he or she means by what he says." Dad paused as if in thought. "I suppose your friendly talk stopped, too, didn't it?"

"Yes."

"Jim is the son of your uncle's tenant farmer. The Dills family are from Jackson County deep in the Smoky Mountains. Garland brought his family here because he has an opportunity to buy his own farm after a few years as a tenant for your uncle. Jim's mother is one-quarter Cherokee, and Garland is a descendant of the family that established the town of Dillsboro on the Tuckasegee River over two hundred years ago. That's near Cullowhee where I went to college."

Dad paused to let that soak in before he continued, "Jim's language and that of all his family is probably the closest to Old English you will ever hear. As for the so-called King's English as Fay says, Jim is probably closer to word choice and pronunciation of it than your teacher." (Fay Medlin was my father's first cousin as well as my seventh- and-eighth grade teacher.)

"It's not Jim's ignorance of language that's at stake here, it's your ignorance of the Dills' history, as well as your ignorance of the history of language, and your bad manners. Interrupting or correcting or teasing others when you know what they mean is low class. You made fun of Jim, and that always hurts. You should never mock anybody's pronunciation or grammar. It's mean in the true sense of the word: degrading, ignoble, base, or paltry. Meanness lacks kindness. It's reluctance to oblige another person."

Dad paused and took a minute to control what seemed to me a rising anger. My father was a patient man who valued the respect people gave our family. "To have friends, you need to be a friend," he said.

I felt his tongue lashing.

After Dad was discharged from the Army at the end of World War I, he worked for ten years as an engineer in the lumber camps of the Northwest. He had told me many things he learned from the Chinese immigrants with whom he had worked in those camps. Once after listening to my aunts decide that the French were the best cooks in the world, my father spoke up and said, "No, you're wrong. The Chinese are the best cooks in the world because they can make a delicious meal out of nothing."

When we were almost home, Dad said, "When you respect people, you can learn from them. Small minds are not open to listening and learning. They judge by their prejudices."

As we neared the house, Dad put his arm around my shoulders and said, "A man is never ashamed to own he's been wrong."

THE WHOLE EARTH

The mules, Tom and Kate, pulled our flatbed wagon beside Mr. Doc Gaddy's tool shed. I had ridden with Dad on the wagon so I could help load the corn planter that Mr. Gaddy had borrowed from my father. It stood next to the disk harrow in the shed.

Mr. Gaddy had seen us coming up the Brooks Branch road and he met us and the mules at his shed.

"Good of you to come and pick up your planter, Buddy," he told my father.

The corn planter was a one-row machine pulled by one mule and guided in a prepared furrow. The single-tree of the mule was connected to the hitch in front of a single, large, narrow iron wheel that cut a grove in the dirt to receive the seed and fertilizer. There were two tall containers on the top of the machine, one for seed corn and the second for fertilizer.

As the planter was pulled in the furrow the mechanism dropped a grain of corn every six or eight inches while it also spread a small stream of fertilizer in the same groove the large wheel cut. Two straight blades, one on each side behind the planting mechanism, plowed the loose soil over the fertilizer and the seed. It was a brilliant invention for planting a large field of corn. So much faster than hand dropping the seed as we did in our vegetable gardens.

When the tanks were filled with fertilizer and seed corn, the planter could be heavy, but I was strong enough to operate it in the field. Even empty, it was too heavy for one man to lift onto the wagon bed.

Mr. Gaddy wasted no time taking the planter handles and rolling it to the wagon. The three of us lifted it onto the flatbed, letting it lie on its side.

After that job was accomplished and before we turned the mules to head home, Doc and my father talked about how many acres each was planting in corn and wheat. In the conversation Doc told Dad that he wanted to purchase some more land. "That over yonder on Brooks Branch and some from the Reynolds' old farm." He waved an arm toward the distant sections.

"Well," Dad said to him, "you have more land now than I could farm by myself. You and Addie don't have children to leave it to."

Mr. Gaddy just looked at my Dad. Dad seemed at a loss for a moment and then he asked, "Doc, how much land do you want?"

"Just what jines me."

As Tom and Kate pulled our wagon and its planter back down the road toward home, I asked Dad, "How much land joins Mr. Gaddy?"

Without looking at me, Dad said, "The whole earth."

PART FOUR

The Gun in Dad's Hands

"Della! Della! Della!" My Dad shouted.

It was a hot August afternoon. Dad was in the bottomland, across the road and below the level of our house, where he was engineering the digging of drainage ditches in Uncle Oliver's field. Uncle Oliver's tenant farmer, Amos Night, and his hired men, Marshall Gregg and Newton Early, were at the ditch digging with their picks and shovels.

Uncle Oliver with his rifle had come to inspect the work and watch for a groundhog that lived somewhere along the stream side. The animal had been helping himself in one of mother's vegetable gardens on that side of the creek.

Mother was busy finishing the Monday wash. Clotheslines in the pasture on the hill above our house sagged with loads of clothes, sheets, and towels drying in the hot sunshine. Two pair of Dad's denim overalls were still drying and fading on the fence that separated the pasture from our yard.

Between the well and our woodyard, the cast-iron wash pot, in which wash water was heated and our clothes boiled, stood over the dying coals. I had helped Mother empty the large galvanized wash tubs of their dirty rinse water, and we had set them back in the well house. They would serve as our bathtubs in the kitchen next Saturday night.

Pete, our beagle, had found his cool spot under the kitchen porch from where he dozed and watched for the twins and me to resume our games. Our play was always woven into the necessary work. We stopped our playing when mother wanted our help wringing out large, heavy, wet sheets. All morning I had added dry wood to the fire under the wash pot to keep the water boiling. Sometimes Mother would let me agitate the clothes in the pot, always warning me not to slosh the water on the fire. While she used the scrub board, she would allow the twins to take turns with the paddle on pairs of Dad's denim overalls. Dean and Dot, my twin sisters, had also taken turns holding the clothespin basket for Mother as she stretched and pinned the wash on the long lines.

∽ ♦ ∾

That afternoon, Dean was at the clotheslines on the hill holding the clothespin bag for Mother while she unpinned and folded the dried sheets and clothes and placed them in her basket.

Before he left the house at noon, Dad had instructed me to drain the water from the milk race in our well house and refill it with cold, well water. Our small, stone well house, built deep into the bank behind the well, was located just off to the side of our kitchen porch. Uncle Glenn, a stonemason and one of Mother's brothers, had laid the stone of the well house before he joined the Army, and he was, on that August day, a prisoner of the Japanese somewhere in the Pacific.

We drew our water with a tall hand pump that stood on a cement lid directly over the well. Dot pumped the water for me that day, filling a second bucket while I carried the first full one into the well house and emptied it into the race. Dot pumped water until I had all the fresh milk, cream, buttermilk, cottage cheese, and butter buckets almost afloat in the water of the race.

I had just shut the well house door when I heard Dad calling Mother.

"Run, see what your father wants," Mother told me as she went on across the porch and into the kitchen with her arms full of clean, dry laundry.

"Hey! Della! Della!" Dad called in a voice of agitation and anxiety. With Pete at our heels, Dot, Dean, and I ran over the yard and across the road to the edge overlooking the bank.

I saw that all the workmen were up out of the ditches, standing and looking toward Mr. Mark's field of wheat stubble. Both Dad and Uncle Oliver were crossing the creek headed in our direction. Uncle Oliver was carrying his rifle.

As Mother arrived at our side, Dad yelled, "Della, get the children in the house. See the dog in Mark's field below the barn!"

From our position on the edge of the road and above

the fields, we could see a large, brown and black collie shaking and staggering sideways, making slow progress toward the gravel road.

Calmly, Mother said, "Let's get Pete into the well house." Pete followed us back to the house and into safety, and mother shut the door on him.

Mother and the girls stood behind the screen door of our kitchen and watched. I went back out into the road and stood near Uncle Oliver and my father.

Having made his way under the old fence and into the road, the dog began his painful progress on toward us. He moved unsteadily as if he were struggling against a strong wind, but it was a perfectly calm day.

"That dog's got hydrophobia," my father said. "See how he walks sideways and appears to be going to fall on his side? He's twitching, very sick, very dangerous."

"Here, Buddy." Uncle Oliver offered his rifle to Dad. It was his 1915 Stevens Hollingblock, single-shot, 22-gauge. "You shoot him."

"No, go ahead. You never miss," my Dad told him. Uncle Oliver always shot the hogs at killing time with that rifle.

"That's at close range when a hog's in the pen," Uncle Oliver argued. "You had military training, Buddy." Uncle Oliver referred to my father's army years during World War I and put the gun in Dad's hands. "I'm not as steady as I used to be," he added.

Dad took careful aim at the dog. Looking at us through bloodshot eyes, the poor animal paused as if he wanted to make a better target. At that moment Dad pulled the trigger. The dog dropped in the dirt at the crack of the rifle.

We waited silently, watching for any movement in the collie, but it twitched no more. Dad told me, "Stay away from that dog. He's just as dangerous dead as he was alive."

Marshall and Amos had arrived beside us in the road with their shovels. Marshall said, "Buddy, we'll bury that dog for you." They were as quick and efficient as their word.

SLAUGHTER TIME

Uncle Oliver raised his gun and took careful aim at Porky, my favorite hog.

While hogs were the prime source of meat for our family, and I had witnessed hog killing on our farm every fall since I was born, I always felt sympathy for the hog. Dad advised us not to give a name to any pig or chicken on our farm because, he said, "No one wants to remember at breakfast that he is eating bacon from 'Porky' or meat of 'Chanticleer' or 'Henny Penny' in the dumplings."

Nevertheless, as I fed the hogs every morning and evening, and brought them water at noon, I gave them names. It's easy to love and admire animals, even those one expects to eat next winter or next Sunday. I knew that I could not eat any beef that had once been my dairy cow—Old Jersey Bell or Brenda. But then, we did not eat beef at our house.

Mr. Dills held Tom, our mule, who was hitched to the small sledge near the hog pen. Uncle Oliver pointed his 1915 Stevens Hollingblock, single-shot, 22-gauge rifle at my Porky. He took his time, waiting for the hog to lift up his head from the trough and look straight at the rifle. It was Dad's and Uncle Oliver's notion that no animal should be made to suffer unnecessarily. Clubbing the hog to death could lose the sweet taste in the meat if the hog grew angry or terrorized before death. Also, bruised meat would spoil rather than cure.

Porky was drinking milk and meal from his trough. Leaning over the edge of the hog pen with his elbow on the top board, his rifle against his shoulder, and his head under the low roof, Uncle Oliver grew tired. He lowered his rifle and stood straight.

"Boys, let's rest a little," Uncle Oliver said into the silence of waiting men. "When the hog finishes his last meal and looks up at me, I'll shoot him between the eyes. He won't know what hit him." In all the years that I witnessed hog killings, Uncle Oliver never had to shoot a hog twice. He never rushed the slaughter.

I took a last look at my hogs. They seemed content slurping the slop we had brought them to keep them quiet. I remembered how these pigs when young squealed with delight as I approached their pen laden with fresh slop, shelled corn, and a bucket of water.

Mother always cleaned any table scraps of bones before we made up the hog feed. Dad insisted that we not feed the pigs any pork leftovers, careful not to make cannibals out of our hogs, even though we knew that one must keep newborn pigs away from the boar or he would eat them. Lassie got to gnaw the ham bones when Mother was at last finished with them.

My hogs were so large and heavy now that they sometimes ate sitting on their rumps near the trough. Grunt weighed at least two hundred fifty pounds and Porky, who seemed more active, was not a pound less. Today they stood and appeared to wonder how they were attracting so much attention.

My mind went back to the day Dad brought the two little pigs home from the stock market. He always selected males, and so Dad called me to help him castrate them while they were small. I had watched the pigs root around in the barn shed while Dad got ready for the operation. It was then that I decided that one of the little pink pigs looked just like Porky Pig of Disney fame. The other one I called Grunt, fitting his attitude and vocabulary.

Dad brought his nail keg from the feed room, a milking stool from the dairy parlor, and his medical supplies: alcohol, kerosene, disinfectant, and his whetstone. He placed them outside the cow stall where the pigs waited. We would take one piglet at a time from the stall and out in the barn lot for the operations.

Dad grabbed a back leg of Porky with his left hand and picked him up, taking the other leg in his right hand. I held the nail keg still while Dad lowered the piglet into the keg head first. We turned the keg on its side and I sat straddle on the keg, holding a hind leg of the pig in each hand, the pig upside down in the keg with his scrotum exposed between his hind legs that I held apart and close to the side of the keg. Porky could not move and his screams would be muffled by the keg and his little fat sides.

Dad sat on the milking stool, took out his pocket knife, selected the small and very sharp blade from among the four blades, rubbed it on his whetstone a few times and then dipped it into the alcohol bottle. "Just pull his legs toward you, son. Put your full weight on the keg and don't turn him lose for anything,"

As I held his hind legs, I watched Dad work. Dad was left-handed, so with his right hand, he pulled the scrotum up tight and rolled the pig's left testicle up tight against the membrane of the scrotum. With the knife in his left hand, he sliced through the membrane and squeezed that first testicle out of its scrotum. He lay down his knife, then pulled the testicle out to the end of the spermatic cord as piglet screamed in pain. Dad cut the spermatic cord near the body and freed the testicle which he tossed to Lassie, our dog, waiting patiently for the fresh meat. Then he repeated the same operation exactly with the second testicle. There was almost no bleeding during the entire operation.

While I still held piglet in the nail keg by his hind legs, Dad rubbed on a disinfectant and saturated the wound with kerosene oil. Then I pulled piglet out of the keg and turned him lose back in the clean cow stall. We performed the same operation on Grunt who grunted constantly and screamed just as loudly as Porky when his spermatic cord was jerked.

৩ ♦ ৶

Dad had chosen a clear and cold late November day for the slaughtering and butchering of the hogs. Dad and Uncle Oliver had waited for cold weather and the right time of the moon. Dad always followed the signs, because if one killed a hog on the new moon, one could not fry the grease out of it. It was the full moon, so that as the moon was shrinking, the meat would shrink and there would be a lot of lard and grease. Mother used lard rather than shortening in cooking.

Early that morning Dad had started a fire under a small pile of hard rocks we had gathered a few days ago from the creek bank for heating the water to scald the hogs. We used a fifty-gallon, iron oil drum that was laid at a steep angle in a depression that we had dug into the ditch near the woodyard. It was now filled with water heated by those rocks from the morning fire, which Dad had shoveled into the water of the oil drum before we took the mule and sledge and the men to our hog pen on the hill above the vegetable garden.

Suddenly into my private thoughts, Porky raised his head up from the trough, his innocent look searching Uncle Oliver's gun barrel, which was aimed right at the center of his skull exactly between Porky's eyes. The rifle cracked. Porky fell dead.

Immediately, my father opened the pen door while he and Mr. Dills reached for the hog's head to pull him out the door, but Porky was much too heavy as dead weight to pull that way. I jumped through the opening above the trough and into the pen and got his tail to pull-push my hog out the door. Grunt stood near the far wall and grunted, "What is this?"

As soon as Porky was on the grass of the pasture beside his pen and the door was closed so Grunt would not wander out, Dad took the butcher knife borrowed from Mother's kitchen and immediately pierced Porky's jugular vein located on the side of the throat about three inches back of the jawbone. The hot blood gushed from my hog spilling what remained of his life in the grass and running down the hillside. He began to shrink even as we watched his blood spill. Who would have thought Porky had so much blood in him?

ALONE IN THE WOODS
WITH KATE

"Your uncle's been gone an awful long time just to get that log," my father said to me. Uncle Taylor, my dad, and I had spent a hot August day on the ridge above the cow pasture at the edge of the mountain forest. We had felled an old oak tree and an aged poplar, sawed them into sections, and hauled them on the sledge to the woodyard. There was only one heavy log remaining on the ridge to be dragged to the woodyard.

The corn crop was laid by. Wheat had been harvested and thrashed. The tobacco was ripening in the hot summer sun. It was much too soon to dig potatoes or harvest apples. The Dog Star, Sirius, had risen in the night sky, but it was not a time of stagnation or inactivity on our farm.

August was the time of year to fill the large woodshed at Grandfather Morgan's home with fuel enough for the coming winter. My grandparents, Aunt Bess and Uncle Taylor, and Great-uncle Gaston all lived in the homeplace. Not only did the Home Comfort Range in Aunt Bess's kitchen demand wood every day, but there were five fireplaces in my grandparents' large home to be fueled during the winter months. By cutting and splitting the wood in the fall we gave it time to dry and make perfect fuel for the cold and wet months ahead.

Prostate cancer was slowly and painfully taking Grandfather Morgan's life. In spite of her advanced arthritis pain and dimming sight, Grandmother kept crocheting doilies for each of her many grandchildren, and asking Aunt Bess to label each doily and put it in the trunk to be handed on "after I'm dead and gone."

After the milking was done, and while the grass was still wet with dew that August morning, Dad and Uncle Taylor, and I had taken the mules and sledge and axes and the two-man cross-cut saw up the ridge into the trees far from the view of the house. Uncle Taylor had chosen an old oak and an aged poplar to fell. Taking turns with Uncle Taylor at one end of the cross-cut saw opposite my father, we three had felled and sawed up the two trees by noon, making them ready for hauling or dragging to the woodyard. There, we would later saw the wood into proper lengths for stove or fireplace and Great-uncle Gaston Cole would split it and store it in the large woodshed.

The morning's work had ceased when we heard Aunt Bess call "DIN-NERRR!" Her voice carried up the mountain ridges and echoed among the hills of the mountain farm. In my mind's eye I could see Aunt Bess step out the kitchen door onto the flagstone walk, cup her hands around her mouth, call "dinner," and return to her kitchen and the care of my grandparents.

The only clock we had on the ridge with us was the watch in the bib pocket of Dad's overalls, but there was no need to check it, because Aunt Bess always called dinner in time for us to take the first sledgeload of wood to the house, wash up and sit down to a hot meal at exactly noon.

On WWNC radio, we heard, "It's high noon in New York and time for Kate Smith." After she sang Irving Berlin's 1938 version of "God Bless America," we listened to Edward R. Murrow report the world news.

At one o'clock, and as a kind of mental relief following the news, Dad and Aunt Bess listened to the fifteen-minute soap opera, "Our Gal Sunday." It always asked the question, "Can this girl from a little mining town in the West find happiness as the wife of a wealthy and titled Englishman?" I had listened often enough to believe the answer was "No."

Uncle Taylor sat in a yard chair nearby and read the *Asheville Citizen.* Uncle Gaston and Grandmother sat in their rockers on the porch. I walked out onto the yard and lay down under the mimosa tree and fell asleep on the thick grass.

Dad had a romantic streak in him. When just a boy, I heard him sing to Mother: "You are my sunshine, my only sunshine. You make me happy when skies are gray. You'll never know, Dear, how much I love you. Please don't take my sunshine away."

At exactly one fifteen, I heard Dad say, "Wake up! Make hay while the sun shines." We collected the team and sledge and headed back to the woods on the ridge.

ھ ◆ ھ

By late afternoon, we had brought all the wood down to the woodyard except one log. It was Uncle Taylor who said, "I'll take Kate back up the ridge and drag that last log in before I quit. It won't take me half an hour."

Over an hour later, my father observed, "Your uncle's been gone an awful long time just to get that log. Go see what's taking him so long."

I jumped across the creek, and ran along the sledge path past the chicken house and the bull pen, through the open gate and started along the old mountain road in the pasture where I met Uncle Taylor limping along behind Kate and the log she was dragging home.

After Kate was unharnessed and put out in the lot with Tom, Uncle Taylor told us how he came to be limping. " I got Kate hooked to the log. You remember how it lay on the hillside. Kate began to pull the log up toward the trail. I was on the lower side of the log. It began to roll toward me, and as I jumped out of the way I stumbled on a root and fell and dropped the reins. I shouted 'Whoa' to Kate. She stopped just as the log rolled on my foot and then on my leg. It pinned me down out of reach of the reins.

"I lay pinned there but glad that Kate and the log had stopped. I knew if I could talk Kate right, she could pull the log uphill and off me. If she pulled toward the trail the log would drag over me.

"I talked Kate into turning uphill and when she was at right angle to the log and facing uphill, I urged her forward, and when Kate pulled, the log rolled back off my leg and foot.

" Kate stood still. I got up and sat on the log a bit. Kate's a good mule."

"What about your leg?" Dad asked.

"Just some skin peeled off. Nothing broke. I'm OK. We'll need to fell two more trees tomorrow."

During Snowflakes

"We get these hogs butchered, we'll have a good supper tonight," Dad said to me as we strained to turn Grunt over in the scalding water. Scalding the hog was the most distasteful part of hog killing for me. Sousing the body in the steel drum of steaming water required backbreaking work. Dad and I rolled it over to loosen the hair. No animal is as heavy as a dead one. It seems to have a greater affinity for earth.

Earlier on that cold November morning, while I cleaned up in the dairy barn, Dad and Mr. Dills had scalded, scraped, and gutted Porky. His open carcass was hanging head down at the well house. Uncle Oliver had returned to the pen and shot Grunt, and we now had this second hog at the scalding drum. We worked in the cold because the freezing temperature would prevent the meat from spoiling until it could be cured.

"Buddy, hold that hog in the hot water just long enough to loosen the hair or the heat will set it," Uncle Oliver cautioned my father.

"Get out of the way, Son," Dad ordered me.

"Garland," he called to Mr. Dills, "Give us a hand. Grab this other leg and let's pull him onto the sledge."

Mother handed me an old knife. Dad and I began

to scrape the black and white hair off in great piles. The smell of wet, steaming, dirty, hog hair in the cold damp air made me work faster. The hot hog's body warmed my fingers.

After Mr. Dills and Dad dipped the hog once more head first into the scalding water, Dad told me, "Work fast. Scrape the head clean." Mother poured hot water from a kettle onto the hog's head and I cleaned around the eyes and ears and snout the best I could. As I scraped around the hog's eyes, I remembered once asking her when I was younger, "Why must I clean the head? Don't we throw it away?"

"I use parts of the hog's head to make liver mush you like so much." She had added, "Some people call it souse meat."

While I warmed my reddened hands at the fire, Dad glanced at the head I had cleaned and said, "We'll have hog jowls and black-eyed peas for New Year's. You remember?" He continued to scrape off the last hairs on the hog's feet. "Did you know," he suddenly asked me, "that there's enough bones in a hog's foot to lay one at every man's door in the county?"

"I don't think there's that many," I bantered.

"There are, if you put the bones at the County Courthouse door," he explained as he admired his work on the hog's feet. "That's every man's door."

"These feet will make sweet meat when I boil 'em," Mother said to me. I knew that we would have hog's feet for supper some evening, or Mother would pickle and can them and we would eat them later in the winter. "But not tonight," I thought. "Tonight we will have my favorite supper that Mother always fixes on hog-killing day."

ℒ◆ℛ

When we had scraped Grunt clean, the wet pink flesh glistened in the light of the fire nearby.

"Hold these legs still for me," Dad said. I watched him cut the skin on the heels of Grunt's back legs to expose his hamstrings.

"Garland, hand me that singletree," he asked Mr. Dills. I held the hog's rear legs as Dad slipped a hook from each end of the singletree to each exposed tendon. (A singletree, sometimes called a whiffletree or whippletree, is the pivoted crossbar to which the traces of a harness are fastened and by which the draft animal pulls a wagon or plow or sledge.)

When we got the hog near the smokehouse, I asked, "How we goin' to lift this heavy hog?"

"Pay attention!" Dad barked. "Be guided with the eye. Watch and learn. It's dullards who have to have everything explained." He hooked the hog's singletree to the rope that was run through a pulley wheel attached to the joist of the floor of the smokehouse above. The other end of the rope he tied to the back of the sledge.

"Garland, urge the mule forward," Dad directed Mr. Dills. When Tom pulled the sledge away, the hog's body rose. Dad guided the singletree to the hook in the joist above. When hanging, Grunt was so large and heavy that his snout reached almost to the cement underneath our feet. At last, he was prepared for butchering.

To Mr. Dills, Dad said, "Garland, take Tom to the barn and remove his harness. Let him have some water and turn him into his stall."

"I'll get a bite to eat at home before I come back," Mr. Dills announced.

After Uncle Oliver had watched the cleaning and hanging of Grunt, he said, "Boys, I'm going home to the fire. It's getting colder. You don't need this rifle anymore." He climbed into his Studebaker truck and drove slowly away up the road.

✑◆✑

Once Grunt was hung with his head down, Mother rinsed the meat free of lose hair and dirt. Dad took out his whetstone from his coat pocket and honed the blade of his butcher knife to a razorsharp edge. I watched as he cut around Grunt's neck at the base of his head and through the throat so that the backbone was ringed completely. Then, he twisted the head off and handed it to me. "Set this on the table in the well house. Lassie could be tempted to gnaw on it."

While we took a break for some hot cider and biscuits by the fire, the remaining blood drained from Grunt's carcass into a large pan that Mother had placed under the headless hog. The second hog was ready to be butchered.

Dad and Mother worked together mostly in silence. After all, they had both butchered hogs since they were young. Knowing that Dad was ready to remove the intestines, Mother placed one of her large galvanized wash tubs on the cement under the carcass. As Mother and I watched, Dad made one long deep cut down the middle of Grunt's belly from crotch to chin, being careful not to cut through the membrane holding the intestines. Then he cut the large intestine free at the anus. He pulled the end out and Mother handed him the string with which he tied the gut shut. Next he cut the gullet at the base of the throat and tied another string tight around it. When he cut the membrane that held the intestines inside the hog, the entrails fell out into the tub.

The sheer beauty of the inside organs always stunned and amazed me. Every organ, neatly in place and alight with colors, glistened in light blues and pinks and dark burgundy, rainbows of light and life. I've never forgotten how clean and bright the meat appeared fresh from the great cavity of ribs and flesh and muscles.

"Pull the tub of guts away," Dad instructed me. Mother replaced the tub I pulled away with another tub, and when I returned to watch Dad, he said, "Put your hands on each side of this cut and hold the sides apart as I finish." He pointed out the different organs as he cut them free and laid them in the clean tub.

"Here's the liver." He laid it in the tub. "See the gall bladder at its side?"

Mother took the organs and put them to soak in water. Dad cut out the lungs, heart, and kidneys. After he trimmed the valves, veins, and arteries off the heart, he retrieved the stomach and small intestines from the entrails' tub, and Mother washed and drained them and set them in water. He also cut off the bladder. As he handed it to me he said, "We can make a balloon for Sister later." I put it on the table in the well house.

The day grew darker under the gathering snow clouds, and when Dad had the two carcasses completely clean, he looked at Mother. "Two hogs killed and ready to cut up, a good morning's work." Then he asked her, "What have we got to eat?"

"I've got hot cornbread in the oven, beans in bacon grease on the stove, and some potatoes baked in the ashes of the fireplace," Mother told Dad. I thought of the basement shelves loaded with cans of jellies, apple sauce, grape juice, tomato juice and tomatoes, beans and crocks of sauerkraut, jars of cider, bins of potatoes and apples, cans of blackberries for pies, peaches, pears, onions and spices hanging from hooks. From the milk race in the well house, Mother took butter, cottage cheese, and whole milk. We were hungry.

I was fifteen. Dad had kept me home from school to help with the killing. After eating, we had about three hours to get the meat ready to grind sausage and render lard before my three sisters would be home from school to help. (I did not know it at the time, but Mother was three months pregnant with my brother.)

While Mother cleared the table and put food away

in the bread warmer over the stove, Dad and I went out to the carcasses hanging in the cold. He cut out the leaf lard, the fat that held the intestines, and dropped it into the pot that I held for him.

Mr. Dills returned to help us. He and Dad took the carcasses down and carried them into the smokehouse where they laid them on the knee-high shelves.

"Bring two chairs and set them by those tubs of entrails," Mother said to me. "We'll trim the fat off the intestines." I took hold of the anus end of the large intestines and as I pulled the guts by Mother, she trimmed off the fat with her knife, careful not to puncture a gut. She added the fat pieces to the pot of fat while I slowly piled the trimmed guts into another empty tub. I knew Mother would render the fat into lard and cracklin's.

I thought about getting my favorite meal after the evening chores were finished. "I can already taste cracklin's in hot cornbread," I told Mother.

We listened to Dad and Mr. Dills cutting up the carcasses in the smokehouse. In the past I had helped Dad with the cutting up. With the ax, he chopped all the way down both sides of the backbone of each hog. He lifted the spine out when the meat fell into two large halves.

Mr. Dills appeared by Mother, holding the tenderloins, "Mrs. Morgan, where should I lay this meat? Buddy said you would know."

"In the sink in the kitchen is probably the best place for now, Garland," Mother directed him.

As he came out from the kitchen, he said, "You all living high on the hog now!"

"We're lucky, Garland," Mother acknowledged his meaning. Then she added, "Marshall would say, 'You're on the pig's back.' He's Irish, you know."

By the time Mother and I were finished trimming the entrails, Mr. Dills had brought down the fatback and put it somewhere in the kitchen.

The school bus arrived. My three sisters, Dot, Dean, and Glennan, got off the school bus and walked up the yard to Mother and me.

"I think we got off at the wrong place," Dot said.

"Welcome home." I meant it with all my heart.

"Get your clothes changed and meet me in the kitchen," Mother told them.

Finished with cleaning the guts, I went to the smokehouse to watch and help Dad and Mr. Dills. After Dad sliced out the ribs and the inside of the middlin' meat, he and Mr. Dills took the ribs and backbones to a clean chopping block in the woodyard. There Mr. Dills held the ribs while Dad chopped them into short lengths. He cut the backbone at each vertebra and put it together with the ribs. "Take these to your mother," he directed me.

As I picked up the heavy buckets of meat, Mr. Dills said, "Buddy, I better be goin'. It's milkin' time."

Dad looked him in the eyes and said, "Garland, we're much obliged for your help. We'll kill your hogs when you're ready."

When I entered the kitchen, Mother looked a bit tired, and she mumbled, "Meat is overwhelming us!" I could see that the table, the sink counter, and the Hoosier cabinet leaf were covered with pans of fresh meat and that a few sausage and fat pots were standing on the floor.

"The shelves are covered in the smokehouse and the well house." I confirmed. "Where are we going to eat supper?" I was getting hungry.

Mother seemed to read my mind. "Tell your father to cut up those hog's heads before you quit."

After Dad cut the shoulders and hams off the middlin's, he trimmed them, adding the steaks of lean to the sausage pots. The four large middlin's, when cured, would be our bacon next winter. They were beautiful lying there on the smokehouse shelves.

As Dad closed the smokehouse door and we started down the steps, cold wind began to spit snow. I remembered Mother's request. "Dad, Mother wants you to prepare the hog's heads before we go to the dairy barn."

He looked at me as if to consider what to do first and then said, "Ask your mother for her largest mixing bowl and bring it to the chopping block."

We took both hogs' heads from the well house to the chopping block where Lassie watched expectantly for a bite of fresh meat. I held a head on the block and Dad chopped off the snout. He pitched it to Lassie who smelled it and then looked as us in disappointment.

Keeping the veil of skin intact around the brains, Dad spooned them out into the large mixing bowl and I returned the bowl to the kitchen counter.

Icy snowflakes swirled around us as we hastened to the barns–me to help Aunt Bess milk the twenty dairy cows and Dad to feed the mules and beef cattle.

✥

When Dad and I entered the warm kitchen after we had finished all the chores, we met the sweet smell of fat being rendered into lard on the stove. Mother and my sisters had somehow cleared the dining table of the many pans and pots of meat. Mother said, "Get cleaned up and come to supper." The day's work in the cold had given me a good appetite.

After we took our places, Mother brought my favorite supper to the table: hot biscuits, honey, and hog brains in scrambled eggs.

Heaven on Earth.

HIS LAST LETTER

"Taylor, do you think you could shave Ernest this morning before the funeral?" Aunt Bess asked. I was standing with them beside the casket on its bier surrounded by flowers in a room on the first floor of the east wing of the house; it had been Grandmother's bedroom before she died. Grandfather's bedroom had been in the west wing.

Uncle Ernest died in a county hospital in Phoenix, Arizona, where he had chosen to live and work some years before, hoping the arid climate would help him fight his advancing rheumatoid arthritis.

It had been over a week since the telegram came with news of his death. The legal arrangements and costs of getting his body embalmed and shipped by rail to Dunn and Groce Funeral Home in Asheville, North Carolina, had been taken care of by Uncle Taylor. In the spring of 1950, the business of shipping his body by rail had taken about nine days. In death, his beard had continued to grow, so his face was showing over a week's stubble of black beard.

"Ernest was always so careful of his grooming and dress," Aunt Bess said as her fingers touched the sleeve of his light gray suit coat before she slid them onto his hand. "Cold as winter clay," she whispered. Uncle Taylor took his arm from around Aunt Bess, and without a word, walked quietly into the hall and turned toward the kitchen wing of the house.

ᵍᵒ ◆ ᵉˡ

Uncle Ernest was the eighth child of thirteen born to my Morgan grandparents. Born in 1892, he was just seven years older than my father. Like Dad, he and his wife, Doris, had first a son and then twin daughters, though I never knew my aunt or my cousins.

Uncle Ernest had met and married Doris while he was head electrician on the building of a stadium in Miami. When the stadium was finished, Uncle Ernest returned to the Morgan homeplace and began building a large modern log home on land Grandfather gave him. He chose the cove beyond the apple orchard and set his house on the hillside above the meadow. Surrounded by tall timber and pastureland with a large garden area, the frame of the house that stood in my childhood was impressive. It was to be a large, two-story log home with covered porches, a two-car garage space in the basement, and a kitchen wing facing the west and garden area.

Uncle Ernest personally selected the trees and felled them for the logs on his own property, and he personally split the oak shingles that roofed the structure. However, I knew it only as the skeleton of what it could have become. The logs were never chinked, nor the hardwood floor laid on the joists. From the spacious living room, a wide stairwell rose to the second-floor bedrooms. Empty window and door openings framed a vista of mountains and hills and sky beyond. From the top story one could see through the framework all the way to basement dirt. When Dad and I needed more space to hang tobacco, we used Uncle Ernest's abandoned dream home.

Before I was born, Doris had arrived from their Florida home with their son and twins. With great pride, Uncle Ernest had taken her to see the building of their new home, but to his dismay, Doris declared that she would not live where she couldn't see her neighbors; it was too quiet and private there. She was a city girl, born and bred, and so Uncle Ernest took her and his children and returned to Florida. Uncle Ernest's work took him to many places, and Doris refused to share his life and dreams. Uncle Ernest came to live alone.

About the time I was born, electric power lines were coming to rural America. Uncle Ernest, as a skilled electrician, was well employed as long as he could travel. Back home in the mountains, he told Grandfather Morgan that he would wire the Morgan home for electricity, the house having been equipped originally for gas lighting. He had explained to Grandfather that he could pull the electric wires through the old gas pipes.

Grandfather had said, "Well, if you wish, but you'll probably find electric lights will be just as unsatisfactory as those old gas lights."

Severe rheumatoid arthritis attacked Uncle Ernest early in his life. He came home from Arizona for a month or two in the summers where he helped Aunt Bess garden and can food and make cider. He was a good cook, and he introduced French toast into the breakfast menu that so long had been biscuits and gravy. Also he kept making improvements in the electrical wiring of the old house. Once I caught him on a ladder repairing a light socket in the ceiling without turning off the power. He told me, "Never try this because I know what I am doing, but you would kill yourself."

I knew him as a very handsome, professional electrician and cosmopolitan man. As a young man, he had made lots of money, and he was generous to his nephews, often handing us a handful of cash from his pocket if one of us was going on a date or to Asheville with friends. Dad told me that he counted thirty-six tailor-made suits in Uncle Ernest's closet when Ernest was a young man still living at home.

As his arthritis grew worse, Uncle attacked it with aspirin. Many times a day he would put a palm full of aspirin tablets into his mouth and drink a glass of water, never saying a word about any pain, but his walk became slow and stiff, and his hands became deformed, almost useless claws. He began reading Christian Science literature searching for a way to reverse his disease.

When he was back in Arizona, Aunt Bess and he corresponded regularly by letters. Great-uncle Gaston would hand Aunt Bess a letter from Ernest just in from the mailbox, and she would stop anything she was doing and read the letter to me, again to Dad or Uncle Taylor, and she would write her brothers and sisters all about Ernest and write him their news. I remember his beautiful penmanship at which Aunt Bess would wonder, "How can he write this beautiful script with those crippled hands?"

∾◆∾

In the kitchen, Uncle Taylor dipped some hot water from the water tank at the end of the Home Comfort Range and poured it into a small gray enamel wash pan. He took down his straight razor, the leather strop, shaving soap mug with brush from the cabinet, and asked me to carry the water and towels back to the casket.

"Joe, son, hold the pan close to the casket," he directed me. Carefully Uncle Taylor placed a towel on the pillow under Uncle Ernest's head, then another over his white shirt collar covering his tie and the suit coat on his chest.

He soaked a washrag in the hot water in my pan, wrung the rag out and placed the hot, damp cloth on Uncle Ernest's cold face and beard for about a minute. After removing the damp rag, Uncle Taylor lathered Uncle Ernest's beard. He unfolded his straight razor and stropped it a few times on the leather to put an even keener edge on the blade.

After he pulled up his shirtsleeves, Uncle Taylor scraped a long smooth swath along Uncle Ernest's cold and bloodless cheek. He wiped the beard stubble and the lather from the razorblade on a third towel, which he had placed on the edge of the casket.

Carefully, he continued shaving until Uncle Ernest's face was clean and smooth. Aunt Bess came into the room and watched Uncle Taylor finish the job, then said, "He looks so much more like Ernest, clean shaven."

Later that morning before the undertakers arrived in the room, all Uncle Ernest's brothers and sisters still living stood near his casket.

Into the silence, Aunt Bess said, "In his last letter, Ernest wrote that he would be coming home in the spring, but. . ." She paused a long moment looking at him all shaved and peaceful in his casket and wiped the tears from her cheeks before she finished her sentence. "I didn't know he meant it this way."

WELCOME TO THE SOUTH

"Columbia, South Carolina," the driver announced as our interstate bus came to a stop at the depot. After he turned off the engine and opened the door, he stood up from the driver's seat, faced his passengers and said loudly, "Negroes move to the back of the bus. We're below the Mason-Dixon Line. Welcome to the South."

He picked up a small valise and left the bus.

That morning, along with seven other newly enlisted Marine recruits, I had boarded the Trailways bus in Raleigh, North Carolina. We had sworn to defend our country and fight for liberty and justice for all. I had volunteered for four years of service to my country, and therefore was presented orders to deliver my "squad" to the Marine Corps Recruit Depot at Parris Island, South Carolina, my first command. It was January 21, 1953, Dwight David Eisenhower's first day as President of the United States.

As I was sitting near the back of the bus among blacks and whites, I noted that few people were leaving the bus and that more than half of the passengers were black, so with other people I got up from my seat and moved forward while all blacks moved to seats in the back two-thirds of the bus.

My new seat position was in the fifth row from the front of the bus. All passengers behind me were black.

The short rest stop completed, a new driver stepped aboard and took a long look at us. His frozen stare at a passenger and his curt command, "All Niggers in the back of the bus," made me notice the middle-aged lady of mixed race sitting two rows forward of me on the right side of the bus next to the window. It was at her that the new driver was glowering and speaking. Well dressed, she had a mink collar on her black coat and she wore gold-rimmed glasses.

Calmly, eloquently and clearly she said, "I boarded this bus in New York City, and I have occupied this seat all the way here. I paid the same amount for my ticket as any other person on this bus, and I am remaining in this seat until I get to Miami."

The short driver turned abruptly, left the bus and walked quickly back into the station. We passengers on the bus remained silent.

Almost instantly, we heard sirens screaming and approaching. Two police cars came to a bouncing stop beside our bus as the sirens whined down. From each patrol car an overweight, uniformed officer rolled from the driver's seat and followed the bus driver into our interstate bus. The driver pointed at the lady, who was obviously half white.

Immediately, the truly red-necked officer with a large beer belly stepped into the aisle beside the lady's seat, reached over the empty seat, and with one hand pulled the lady's glasses from her face and pitched them to the floor behind him. He then slapped her very hard across the face, first with the palm of his right hand and again on the other cheek with the back of his hand. He took hold of the front of her blouse and pulled her toward himself.

The other officer, equally large with rotund stomach, stood near the first officer in the aisle. Then the policeman took hold of the woman's coat with the mink collar and lifted her bodily from her seat and shoved her into the grip of the second officer.

At no time did either officer say anything. The woman did not cry out nor strike back at either officer as one pulled and the other shoved her off the bus and stuffed her roughly into the back seat of the nearest patrol car.

Immediately, both cars, again with sirens screaming, pulled away. It did not take more than one or two minutes for the arrest from the time the police arrived and the time they pulled away from our bus and the station. She was taken without her glasses or any other items she had with her. I saw no one remove her luggage from the bus.

The new bus driver, with a smug look, said nothing to us as he climbed into the driver's seat, started the engine and turned the bus slowly back toward U.S. highway 1.

My heart pounded. Whites were in the minority there. Hundreds of black people stood four deep along the bus depot wall silently watching as our bus pulled away. Not one passenger, including us new recruits still in civilian clothes, spoke or moved from his seat.

That beautiful American woman was legally arrested. Those ruthless, uniformed men were the enforcers of the segregation laws of the land. My notions of liberty and justice for all, and my notions of the integrity and honor of my government clashed with the harsh reality of America.

With the lady's seat empty, our bus picked up speed as we traveled on toward Parris Island.

THE SHADOW OF DEATH

Aunt Carrie had The Sight.

With the brevity and certainty of a seer, she would simply "forecast" something that she knew was going to happen, but she suffered the fate of Cassandra. No one took her warnings seriously or "paid her any mind." It would be only after the event happened that someone would remember that Aunt Carrie had said it would come to pass.

My father and I spent many days working on Aunt Carrie and Uncle Oliver's farm, and I remember the comment she made one bright morning as Uncle Oliver, my father, Bud Bonnom, and I were leaving the yard to work in the hayfield. Aunt Carrie said, "It'll rain this afternoon." Dad looked up at the clear-blue sky. Uncle Oliver, who was hard of hearing, just walked on toward the field. "The radio said there's a thirty percent chance. That's a lot of rain!" she added in her defense and chuckled at her own joke.

We didn't rush getting up the hay. However, around three o'clock that afternoon while we stood under the barn shed watching the waterfall pouring from the tin roof, it was Bud Bonnom who remembered, "Carrie said it'd rain today."

Time has proven to me that Aunt Carrie had the gift of intuition, the faculty of knowing without the use of rational processes.

A few years later as I sat at my desk in Washington, D.C., the Sergeant Major called across to me, "Morgan, this call is for you. It's your mother. I'll transfer it to your phone."

As my phone rang, I became aware that a silence fell over the office. None of the men in headquarters knew that my parents did not have a telephone, but still they sensed that tragedy lurked in my call. At the sound of the Sergeant Major's voice and the sight of his raised hand, palm open, my office mates stopped typewriters and conversations and waited quietly, listening to my end of the phone conversation.

"Mother, this is Joe," I spoke into the phone. Then I listened while she told me that Uncle Oliver had been killed a few hours before. And she told me that Aunt Carrie wanted me to be one of his pallbearers.

When I said to Mother, "I'll need to apply for leave," the Sergeant Major who was still watching me and listening to my words, from three desks away, said loudly, "Tell your mother your leave request is approved. And while she's on the phone, tell her you can leave Washington this afternoon." He knew that I kept my '47 Chrysler parked beside the barracks on the street side within view of our office windows.

Before the Dunn and Groce hearse delivered Uncle Oliver's body back home in his casket, it was Aunt Bess and Mother who told me what had happened that fateful day.

"Your Aunt Carrie," Aunt Bess began, "awakened that morning with an awful feeling of inevitable doom and destruction and ruin. She asked your uncle not to go out in the fields but just to sit on the porch with her and let the tenant farmers put up that field of hay. But your Uncle Oliver argued that the hay was ripe and ready and just a few loads would get the job done. Carrie begged him to wait until your father could help him and Taylor do the work." My father had taken Uncle Oliver's '37 Studebaker truck to Cullowhee to bring my sister Freida home from college.

Mother inserted, "It was just that little patch of hay above the house on that steepest part of the field." Uncle Oliver had driven his new Ferguson tractor and the new large trailer Dad had built for him onto the field, and Uncle Taylor, husband to Aunt Bess, had worked with Uncle Oliver that morning loading and hauling the hay. Uncle Taylor had pitched the shocks of hay onto the trailer while Uncle Oliver had driven the tractor from shock to shock. The morning work had gone well. By noon they had left a nearly finished load of hay at the edge of the field and had come to the house to eat.

"After dinner," Aunt Bess told me, "Carrie begged your uncle to let that last load of hay wait for your father's return to help. She cried as she pressed him to leave it alone for later, but her tears and fears were ignored by Oliver." Mother blew her nose and Aunt Bess wiped her tears away with the hem of her apron.

"It was like Calpurnia begging Caesar not to go to the senate on the ides of March," Aunt Bess said. "Oliver wanted to finish, and he promised Carrie that he would come and sit on the porch with her just as soon as he and Taylor loaded those last shocks onto the trailer."

But it was not to be. Within twenty minutes after his leaving Aunt Carrie, Uncle Oliver lay on the hillside, crushed to death.

For over seventy years Uncle Oliver had farmed successfully and safely with teams of mules. He was just learning how to handle his new Ferguson tractor. In the far corner of the steep hillside, Uncle Oliver had turned his tractor uphill pulling the heavily loaded trailer. The front wheels of the small tractor had risen off the ground in the turn.

An experienced tractor driver would have simply guided the tractor by the brake pedals on the large rear wheels. Fearing the tractor would flip over backward, Uncle Oliver jumped off the tractor on the lower side of the machine and fell down into the stubble.

The driverless tractor spun toward him. A large tire rolled over his chest, followed by the trailerload of hay careening on its way down the slope.

Before sunrise that morning, Aunt Carrie had seen the shadow of death.

BURN-SCARRED HANDS

It was early New Year's morning and I had not had my breakfast when Mother said, "Joe, run this dish of food over to Anner and Ellie."

"Why can't Dot or Dean take it?" I complained.

Mother paused in her kitchen work, sat down in a table chair, and looked me in the eyes at my level.

"Anner and Ellie believe it's good luck to have a man as their first visitor in the new year, and they believe it's bad luck to have a woman as a first visitor." She paused and let me digest her words.

So one of the twins should not go. I couldn't have been more than six years old, but it was encouraging to be considered able to do a man's work.

"Do you believe that?" I asked Mother.

"No, of course I don't, but what matters right now is that Miss Anner and Miss Ellie believe it, and they are our neighbors."

I took the dish and started for the door.

"Be sure to wish them a Happy New Year," Mother reminded me.

As I walked into the Daves' yard, I met Mr. Mark coming from his barn.

119

"Well, it's Joe Boy!" he exclaimed. "Come on in by the stove." He took me into the kitchen wing. I held out my dish and said, "Mama sent this for you. Happy New Year."

Ellie peered at me through her thick glasses and said, "It's Joe." Then she took the dish and set it beside a set of scales on her Hoosier cabinet leaf. She put her hand over her mouth and giggled.

"You're our first visitor this year," she said. "You'll bring us good luck all year, ain't it?"

She called, "Anner, look who's here this morning! Deller's sent us some black-eyed peas and hog jowl for New Year's."

When Anner came into the kitchen, she said, "Ellie, give Joe a piece of your pound cake."

"I ain't had breakfast yet," I said, "and Mama said to hurry home."

"Then you just take the whole cake with you," Ellie said. "I baked it for Mark, but I'll bake him another. Give me somethin' to do today, ain't it?"

"Mark's mighty fond of Ellie's cakes," Anner told me.

✺ ◆ ✺

When I placed it on the table at home, my Dad said, "Now that's a real pound cake!"

"Why is it called a pound cake?" I asked.

"Because it's got a pound of flour, a pound of butter, and a pound of eggs in it," Mother explained. "Ellie puts lemon in it, too."

As the years passed, it became my New Year's Day job to visit Anner and Ellie early in the morning.

Soon after Miss Anner died, Mark and Ellie asked Ott Duckett to build them a new house. They stored most of their furniture in the hay barn and moved their beds and the kitchen into a clean, old, unused dairy barn.

It was summer and we laughed and talked and visited the new house site about every day. I believe it was one of the happiest times of their lives, because Ellie soon after began to lose her sight.

Mr. Duckett tore down their grand, old clapboard house and built a modern three-bedroom home with a large farm kitchen convenient to a new wash and well house. However, Mr. Mark said there was no use finishing the inside bathroom because they would use the outhouse always.

◈ ◆ ◈

I came home on leave during the Korean War. When Mr. Mark saw me in our yard, he called over from his barn, "Joe, Ellie's got your cake ready."

I met Mr. Mark in the field, and as we walked together to their warm, new house, he drawled slowly, "I told Ellie I saw your car come in early this mornin'."

I had driven from Washington, D.C., through the night and had arrived home about milking time.

Ellie stood in her kitchen, one hand on the edge of the sink. The bib of her long apron was soiled with food stains and the left corner had snuff smeared on it where she wiped her mouth. Strands of her golden hair streaked with gray hung limp outside the loose bun pinned on the back of her head.

When I said, "Hello, Ellie, it's Joe," she smiled and shuffled a step toward me in a pair of old tennis shoes. She kept one burn-scarred hand on the counter edge and said, "You're home from the war, ain't it?"

I took her other hand with burn marks on it, too, and said, "No, Ellie, I ain't home from the war yet. I'm just on furlough."

"Yea," she replied absently and then she said, "I baked you a cake. You and Mark allis liked my cakes, ain't it?"

"Oh yes, you know we do."

"Mark took it out for me. It's on the counter there, ain't it?"

The cake was under a dish towel on wax paper. It was a rich yellow, another real pound cake.

"I knowed you'd come," she began, "but I ain't no count no more, just cook a little for Mark, ain't it."

"Ellie," I said, "It's such a large cake, I'll take just half and then you and Mark will have some too."

She put a hand over her snuff-stained mouth and giggled, "Mark said it looked like a right good cake, ain't it?"

As I left, I wished Ellie Happy New Year.

About the Author

Joe Richard Morgan left the western North Carolina mountains to serve in the United States Marine Corps during and after the Korean conflict.

A teacher who has taught language, literature, and writing for over forty years, Joe Morgan has been selected twice by his colleagues as teacher of the year and has received the Illinois Governor's Award for Excellence in Teaching.

Joe was one of the last John Hay Fellows. He has received five grants from the National Endowment for the Humanities and a Rockefeller Foundation Grant to study philosophy and humanities in secondary education. Dr. Morgan received his PhD in English Literature from Stafford University, London, UK.

Joe Richard Morgan is the author of *Potato Branch: Sketches of Mountain Memories.* He has two daughters and a son and lives with his wife, Milli, in Mars Hill, North Carolina, and in Bluffton, South Carolina.